Snake Oil

Jay Lang

Print ISBNs
Amazon Print 9780228624417
LSI Print 9780228624424
BWL Print 9780228624431

BWL Publishing, Inc.

I0584400

*Books we love to write ...
Authors around the world.*

http://bwlpublishing.ca

Chapter One

Surrounded by the blue glow of night, Sylvie blinks to clear the blood from her eyes. As her head rests on the broken slats of the wooden steps, she concentrates on the white, peeling railing above and strains to reach it, but she's too weak. Feeling hopeless, she shifts her focus to her constricted chest and takes slow, shallow breaths, praying someone comes before he reaches her and finishes what he started.

* * *

I never get used to the smell of this place. A bouquet of dime-a-bucket perfume, mixed with the ever-present caustic stench of industrial cleaner.

As I walk quickly down the long corridor, fluorescent lights buzzing overhead, I think about my parents and the sacrifice they made for me to be here. Thankfully, they finally got their wish and retired to Scotland, where all their family and friends live. Though, I must admit, I do feel a sense of trepidation about being in Canada alone. Even though I was born here and have called nowhere else home, without waking up to Mom making breakfast in the kitchen and Dad reading the paper in his La-Z-Boy, I feel somewhat displaced.

Late again, I grab the cold knob and push the door open. Twenty-odd students stare back at me as I search for an available seat.

I don't like it here. Everyone reminds me of robots, even the professors. I would rather be outdoors, in a more organic and breathable environment, than stuck in this institution. Thankfully, I am only taking three courses this semester, so I should be able to focus more on each class and up my GPA.

I spot an empty chair between a girl with blue dreadlocks and a guy with rainbow stickers covering his binder. As soon as the prof starts his monotone lecture, my mind wanders to Tessa Waters, my childhood friend and roommate in the residential building. She's been on me to go with her to an off-campus party.

When I was living at home, I never went out at night. My parents had a curfew for me and strict house rules, but they didn't need them; I was a hermit and, because of it, I never had many friends. Now I'm living with countless wild, hormonal students, and all I hear about are parties and get-togethers.

I'm not anti-social. I just prefer to spend my nights curled up with a good book, or surfing the internet. Besides, I'm at least three years older than ninety percent of the other students, and I find most of them immature and annoying.

After high school, I had taken a few years off to work in the hardware store owned by my and Tessa's parents. It was only when my mother and father started talking about moving back to Scotland that I considered going to university, as I couldn't imagine moving away from Canada. Plus, I can't live with my mother and father all of my life. Their move gave me no other choice than to make it on my own. Though, thankfully, they're financing my education.

After what feels like hours, the class ends. I grab my books and head out to the hall, where a sea of students crowds me as I maneuver my way to my next class.

I'm just about to take a seat at the back of the classroom when I hear my name being called. I look up and see Tessa, my roommate.

She pats the seat next to her. "Come and sit over here."

I walk to the front of the room and take a seat next to her. Her hair is in a messy bun and she's wearing a pair of tights and one of my tops.

"I hope you don't mind, but all of my clothes were dirty, so I borrowed one of your shirts."

"It's fine. However, you should know that there's this amazing new invention called the washing machine."

Tessa laughs. "Oh really? Never heard of it. I'll have to check it out."

The professor walks in, an older man with thinning grey hair and thick glasses. He starts to address the class about our daily assignment, and Tessa leans over. "You know, it's Friday night," she whispers. "A bunch of us are heading to a party at Cultus Lake. You should come."

I shake my head. "I need to catch up on a lot of homework. I think I'll just stay in and—"

"Don't be such a stick-in-the-mud, Sophie. You live like a grandma and you're only twenty-three. Live a little."

I sigh, beyond tired of this conversation. "If I say yes, will you promise to never bother me about going to parties again?"

She grins. "I swear it!"

Later that day, I'm in my bedroom, waiting for Tessa. A cool autumn breeze seeps in through my open window, and I shiver. The door opens and she walks in, holding a dress in each hand. "Which do you think I should wear?"

"To an outdoor party by the lake? I'm thinking you'll freeze your butt off. Why

6

don't you wear something more practical, like jeans and a sweater? That's what I'm putting on."

Tessa grimaces. "Oh, no. Please tell me you're not going to dress like my mother tonight. Frumpy and boring."

"Look, all that should matter to you is that I've agreed to go. I didn't say anything about freezing."

Tessa shakes her head. "Well, at least you have all that long, blond hair. It's hard for you to look ugly."

* * *

After we park, we walk along the lake toward a blazing fire pit on the beach. Tessa is holding onto my arm as she tries not to stumble in her restricting tight dress and stiletto heels.

"So, how long do we have to be here?," I ask. "I really want to get some homework done tonight."

"We've just got here, and already you're wanting to leave?"

As soon as we reach the crowd of about fifty partygoers, a guy with his hat on backward and an open shirt walks up to us. "Hey, ladies. Can I get you a drink?"

Tessa nods and follows him to a half-buried cooler in the sand. She returns, stumbling on her heels, and hands me a beer.

I hate the smell and taste of alcohol, so I never drink. My parents had Christmas parties at our house, where they would have an open bar for the guests. In the morning, when helping my mother clean up, I'd nearly barf at the stench of stale booze from the half-drunk glasses. "I'm driving, so I can't drink this." I try to hand the beer back to her.

"Sophie. If this is the only time you're gonna come out with me, then at least have one drink."

I sigh deeply, knowing that she won't stop nagging unless I appease her.

Tessa and I slowly walk through the crowd of half-drunk partiers. She looks over at me, eyes sparkling. "See? Isn't this fun?"

Her idea of a good time and mine are very different. Most of the girls here are wearing two layers of thick makeup and resemble mannequins more than humans. The males in the crowd are ridiculous, hollering and screaming while doing dumbass things like chugging booze through a hose, or sucking on a huge bong.

Finally, we find a log at the water's edge and sit down. Tessa kicks off her shoes and finishes her beer.

Across the lake are beach homes with lights on that flicker across the water. I think about how pissed the homeowners must be, putting up with all the noise from the party. It wouldn't surprise me if the cops got called to break up the mob.

Tessa stands again, and pulls me with her. It isn't long before she engages a group of guys in conversation. As soon as she takes her attention off me, I dump my beer out on the sand.

"Let me guess," a voice from behind me says. "That wasn't your drink of choice?"

I quickly turn to see a beautiful guy wearing a tank top and jeans. His hair is shiny black, and he has full sleeve tattoos on each muscular arm. I swallow hard, then quickly look down at my feet.

"Or maybe," he continues, "you're the party chaperone. You're here to get rid of all \the alcohol so everyone behaves."

"Not likely."

"So what are you doing here, if you're not drinking?"

"I was talked into coming by my roommate, Tessa." I turn to where she was standing, but she and the group of guys she was talking to are now gone. "She was just here a minute ago."

He grins. "What's your name?"

"Sophie." I avoid his gaze. My hands start to shake, so I pull my sleeves down to cover them.

Then, someone from down the beach hollers. The stranger waves at the person, then quickly grabs my hand and kisses it. "Nice to meet you, Sophie. I guess we'll see you around." And he turns and walks down the beach.

As soon as he's gone, I force a deep breath to settle my nerves. *Wow. Who the hell was that? I've never seen anyone that gorgeous, especially not someone who wanted to talk to me.*

Suddenly, Tess appears. "Who was that?"

I shrug. "Beats me."

"You didn't ask for his name?"

I shake my head and look in the direction he was walking, but he's gone.

"Come on." Tessa tugs on my sleeve. "I met these really cool guys who race cars. Let's go talk to them."

Reluctantly, I follow Tessa into the crowd.

After a half-hour of watching Tessa's new acquaintances act like total idiots—and watching my getting-drunk-fast roommate flirt with them—I tell her that I want to go home.

"Aw, come on. The party's just getting started."

Suddenly, one of the idiot guys lunges forward and picks me up in his arms. "You know what you need?" he says, breathing into my face the pungent odor of whatever he's been drinking.

"Let me down," I holler.

"You need to go for a swim!" He heads toward the lake.

"Are you crazy? You'd better not throw me into that water. Put me down, you jackass!"

Tessa yells and makes a half-assed attempt at freeing me from my captor, but gets distracted by the guy beside her and forgets all about me. I kick my feet and continue to holler, but the idiot is obviously too drunk to care; he just keeps walking toward the lake.

"I swear, if you don't put me down now, you're going to be in serious trouble."

The brute laughs. "Oh really? What are you going to do to me?"

As soon as I hear his feet splash in the water, I know there's nothing I can do. I squeeze my eyes shut, and just as I feel him get ready to toss me in, a loud male voice booms from behind us. "Hey, dipshit. Let her go!"

It isn't until the thug swings around to see who's hollering that I see him. It's the same guy that talked to me earlier.

"I said, let her go!" he repeats.

The thug backs out of the water, and the arms around me loosen. I squirm and push free. Finally on my feet again, I back away as the two men get closer to each other. I can feel the tension in the air and the last thing I want is a fight over me. I quickly move between them and put my arms out. "It's all good. I'm fine, and this doesn't need to go any further."

11

The drunk guy that was manhandling me only moments ago glares at the dark-haired stranger. "Hey, man. Mind your own business. I was just having a little fun."

"It didn't look like she was having fun to me."

Then, I see Tessa run toward us. "What's going on, Sophie?"

"Nothing. Everything is fine. Right, guys?"

Tessa clues into the situation as she approaches and grabs the thug's arm. "Come on. Your friends want to talk to you."

At first, the guy doesn't budge. Eventually, though, he shrugs and walks back toward the fire.

I exhale loudly and look at the stranger. "That was intense. Thanks for coming to my rescue. It would've sucked to be thrown into the cold water."

"Don't mention it, Sophie. I'm just glad I happened to be walking by and saw you."

"So, what's your name? You know mine, and I don't know yours."

He smiles. "Brandon."

"Well, Brandon, I owe ya one."

"Are you coming?" Tessa yells from up the beach. "I'm ready to leave now."

Now she wants to leave. It figures.

"That's my roommate. I guess we're leaving."

"That's good. A girl like you shouldn't be out here mixing with a bunch of low-lifes, anyway. As you just experienced, it's not safe."

I see Tessa making her way toward us at the water's edge. Not wanting her to say something embarrassing in front of Brandon, I say goodbye and walk to meet my drunk roomie.

Chapter Two

I awaken to eerie squeaks as the branches from the tree outside scratch against my window. I look out and watch the bright red and yellow leaves twirl in the wind. Lying back down on my pillow, I'm thankful it's the weekend and I don't have any classes to run to.

"Sophie, are you awake?" Tessa yells from the other room.

I sigh. *So much for sleeping in.*

As I get out of bed and grab my robe, my mind flips back to last night, and to meeting the beautiful Brandon. I think about what he said: *"A girl like you shouldn't be out here mixing with a bunch of low-lifes."*

What did he mean by that? Did he think I was a prude? That I didn't fit in with the crowd? Or were his words meant as a compliment?

Either way, it doesn't matter now. He's gone, and I'll probably never see him again.

I go to Tessa's room. From within a cocoon of blankets, she asks if I have anything for a headache. After getting her two Aspirin and a bottle of water, I get dressed and make a smoothie before going back to my room and hitting the books. Later in the morning, I hear the shower turn on after Tessa finally gets out of bed.

The day progresses much like every other. I do homework for a few hours, have some lunch, then do my laundry from the past week. Not surprisingly, Tessa has managed to hide hers in with mine. Knowing there's no point in bringing it up with her—she'll just laugh as though it was a big joke—I just put her clean laundry on her bed.

My father always told me that I need to be more assertive and stand up for myself, but I hate confrontation. I'd rather take the road of least resistance.

* * *

A bouquet of aromatic spices fills the room as Tessa removes the lids from our Indian take-out. Curry is an acquired taste, and since I grew up eating my mother's traditional Scottish cuisine, I find spicy foods challenging. I put on a compilation disc of soft classical music before joining Tessa on the couch to eat.

She makes a face. "Do we really have to listen to this drab music? Every time you play it, I have to fight to stay awake."

I giggle. "You need a bit of diversity, Tess. Besides, classical music is food for the soul."

"If this shit is food for the soul, I'm going on a diet."

My mouth is burning after I finish a plate of screaming hot Rista, a red curry dish with meatballs, saffron, and whatever flame accelerant they marinade it in. "So," Tessa says, after I get up to grab a glass of water. "That guy I saw you with twice last night."

"What about him?" I drink half the cup.

"Did he tell you his name or where he's from?"

"His name is Brandon, but I have no idea where he's from. He looked about thirty, so he's most likely not part of the university crowd."

"Too bad. He was scrumptious. Do you think you'll run into him again?"

"I doubt it. Considering how much I go out, there's probably no chance we'll ever cross paths."

She grins. "Oh, well. There are plenty more hot guys out there."

"Yeah, but not like him. As soon as I looked at him, I turned into Jell-O."

"He was a special kind of hot, that's for sure. Maybe you should come back to the lake next weekend. I hear there's going to be one last beach bash this season. Maybe you'll see him again."

"Nice try, Tess. But no thanks. With my luck, one of those drunk yard apes will succeed in throwing me into the lake, and Brandon won't be there to rescue me."

"Well, you've got a whole week to think about it."

"What you mean is, I have a whole week for you to try to talk me into it."

* * *

With my laundry finished and everything I reserved to get done on the weekend completed, I brave the crisp fall wind and go for a walk around campus. When I get back to our unit, Tessa is talking on her cell in the living room. I overhear her debating about something, then sounding disappointed before she swears and hangs up.

"Everything okay?" I ask.

"Yeah, but this guy I've been hanging out with is busy tonight, which translates to 'he's got someone else he's screwing.'"

"I'm sorry, Tess. But I've seen the guys you've dated, and most of them…"

"Most of them *what*?"

"Well, I just think they don't hold you in high esteem, is all."

"Do you want to repeat that in English?"

17

"What I'm trying to say is that they don't respect you. They see you as a booty call."

Tess jumps up. "So, I'm a slut?"

"No. Of course not. I just think that they're not the right kind of guys for you. They seem pretty non-committal and shallow."

Tessa stares at me. I can see in her eyes that she's trying to figure out if I've insulted her or if my intentions were meant to help her.

"Tessa, I care about you," I say gently. "I think you're a pretty girl with lots to offer someone. All I'm saying is that you can afford to be choosy."

And with that, Tessa relaxes and sits back down on the sofa. A few minutes pass before she talks again. "Let's forget about stupid men for the rest of the evening. Do you want to go to a movie or something?"

I don't want to go out in the worst way, but I know she's feeling down about being rejected by one of many losers she dates. "Sure. I'd love to go to a show."

While Tessa peruses the internet to find out what's playing, I have a quick shower and get dressed. When I return to the living room, she's wearing a black mini-dress and has her hair and make-up done.

"Wow, you're pretty dolled up for a movie."

Tessa looks at me with a fake sad expression, one she's given me whenever she's about to disappoint me. "You're gonna hate me, Sophie. But my guy called, and he's changed his mind. It looks like I'll be going out with him after all."

I should've known. Nothing is more important to her than the attention of the opposite sex. She'll do anything to get it or keep it, even if it means abandoning any sense of self-restraint.

"Don't worry about it," I tell her. "Go have fun."

Once Tessa has left, I sit down on the couch and stare at the wall. Even though initially I wasn't into going out, I got in the mood while getting ready. So, instead of just sitting here, I decide to go to the Asian market in downtown Abbotsford to find some inspiration for a new dish to make. Cooking is a passion of mine that I don't get to indulge in that often.

* * *

Hard rains fall across the Lower Mainland, with Abbotsford and the Fraser Valley getting the worst of it. It doesn't matter where I go—the grocery store, the library, the post office—the main topic of conversation is how unfortunate we are because of the wet weather. I feel like shouting, *Come on people, wake up. We do in fact live in a rainforest*, but I don't. I simply smile and nod, even though I love

19

the rain. I always have. I find it soothing and cleansing somehow.

Though, I admit that driving in a downpour can be challenging, especially with the omnipresent fair-weather drivers that panic and ride their brakes when the road is wet. I remember vacationing with my parents in Scotland one year and it rained the whole time. The weather was bad, but the drivers behaved and were the polar opposite of here. They zoomed around the winding roads at normal speeds and thought nothing of it.

It's been two weeks since Tessa took me to the party at the lake. Surprisingly, she hasn't pushed for me to attend any more. In fact, since the lake, she's only been home for a total of four nights. Sometimes I see her in the evenings when she comes home to take a quick shower and grab a bag of clean clothes, but other than that, I've had the unit to myself. She texted me late last night and said that she needs to talk to me about something, and she'll be home at 8PM. I really hope she's not going to ask me for money again.

It's 5:30 now, so I decide to take the next couple of hours to finish up some English lit homework before Tessa shows up and I get distracted.

I wake with the heavy textbook lying on my chest and a pen in my hand. Glancing over at the digital clock on the stove, I see that it's 10:30 PM. I passed out while doing my homework. I quickly grab my cell and look for any messages from Tessa. There aren't any.

I get up and make a bowl of instant noodles in the microwave, then sit down and message her. It takes about a half hour for her to reply that she's sorry she's late, but something came up. Then, she messages that she's on her way and should be here soon. I laugh out loud, knowing that even though her intentions may be on point, she's as tardy as hell.

Finally, at midnight, in waltzes Tessa. She's wearing a wet hoodie with the hood pulled low on her head, concealing her eyes.

"Hey, Tess. You made it."

"Yeah. I'm sorry I'm late—again. You wouldn't believe the time I've been having." She scans the stack of unopened mail I put on the counter for her. Then, she grabs a can of pop from the fridge and walks over, flopping down beside me on the couch. Now that she's in close proximity, I get a clear look at her eyes, which are bloodshot and ringed with dark circles.

"Wow, Tess. You look like a raccoon."

"I know. I haven't been getting much sleep lately."

"That's not good. I don't know how you're managing classes when you don't rest and don't come home to study."

"Well, that's kind of the reason I wanted to talk to you." She doesn't meet my eye.

I take a deep breath and prepare myself.

"You see, I haven't really been going to my classes."

"At all?"

She shakes her head, then takes a swill of her drink. "I kind of got hooked up with this trucker guy, and he's been taking me on road trips. Last night we were in Alberta."

"I hope you know what you're doing. If you fail your courses, that's a lot of wasted cash that your parents came up with. Not to mention, you're seriously affecting your GPA."

"Yeah, I know. But I'm not telling you all of this so you can nag me or give me a lecture."

I sigh. "Fine. Then why are you telling me?"

She finally makes eye contact. "Because I've decided to quit university and go on the road full-time."

I can't believe what I'm hearing. Even for Tessa, this is probably the pièce de résistance of stupid decisions.

My first instinct is to try and dissuade her from making a catastrophic mistake, but something tells me my efforts would fall on deaf ears, so I just sit and stare ahead.

"I'm sorry, Sophie, but I'm going to be moving out, too."

"Yeah, that's kind of obvious, considering you can't live in res if you're no longer a student."

Tessa tries to make small talk as she finishes her drink, but I'm too busy trying to digest her news to respond.

We sit in uncomfortable silence for a few more minutes before Tessa gets up, pulls her suitcase from the hall closet, and takes it into her room to pack.

Chapter Three

There's a hollow feeling to the unit since Tessa left. Though, I have to admit, I've gotten a lot of studying done without her constant interruptions.

I hope she's okay out there with her new trucker boyfriend. My parents called me about a week after Tessa left; apparently, her parents are freaking out, thinking she's lost her mind. I've texted her a few times, but all I get back is a thumbs-up emoji.

It's a weeknight, and I'm deep into homework when there's a hard rap at the door.

Leaving the security chain on, I open the door a few inches. One of the girls from the neighbouring unit smiles through the crack. "Hey, Sophie. I'm Lacey. I heard about Tessa moving out. I liked her a lot. We had a lot of classes together."

I nod, not knowing how else to respond.

"Anyway, my roomie got two tickets to this cool band that's playing at *The Dark Room* tomorrow night, but now she can't make it. I really want to go, but not by myself. I was wondering if you wanted to buy her ticket and come with me?"

She's bubbly and sweet, but all I can think is, *why is she asking me?* I never hang out with any of the other residents. Maybe she already asked a bunch of people and they said no. "I'd like to, Lacey, but I've got tons of homework to catch up on. Sorry."

We say our goodbyes, and as I close the door, I think about how much time I've been spending alone since Tessa left. I've surpassed my title of a hermit and have been rapidly heading toward becoming a recluse.

I quickly open the door and yell after Lacey: "Hey. On second thought, maybe I can go with you."

Lacey turns and grins. "Awesome! I'll pick you up tomorrow at nine."

* * *

Electric energy fills the crowded basement club as the audience sings along with the band. The walls are covered in cheesy Christmas lights and there are neon ropes under the small stage.

"Who are these guys again?" I yell over the booming music.

"They're called Dark Rider. They're out of Seattle. Aren't they great?" Lacey dances in place.

"I'm going to stand at the back by the bar."

"No!" Lacey latches onto my wrist. "Let's go to the front and dance."

She pulls me behind her through the mob and to the front of the stage. I'm bumping into people, spilling their drinks, and stepping on their feet as I'm yanked along. Between the huge speaker cabinets and directly under the lead singer, whose mohawk reminds me of a porcupine, we dance to the next few songs.

When the singer stops to talk to the crowd, I take the opportunity to make my way to the back of the room. Thankfully, Lacey doesn't notice me leaving.

In front of the long bar are tall stools. I wait until someone gets up, then quickly grab a seat. I feel flushed from the dancing, and from how hot it is in here. When the bartender notices me, I order a soda water with lemon, then turn to watch the band.

"I like the way you dance," a voice says from behind me.

I quickly turn. Immediately my chest tightens, and I feel a trembling in my legs. "It's you."

Brandon smiles as he sits on the stool next to me. "What are you doing here?"

I laugh. "I have no idea. What about you?"

"I like the band, so I thought I'd check them out."

I nod.

We sit in silence for a few more minutes as we watch the band. Finally, I work up the nerve to ask him a question, though I'm too chicken to look at him. "So, how many times have you seen them play?"

When there's no response, I turn to see that he's gone. I scan the room, but can't see him anywhere.

That was weird. I can't believe he left without saying goodbye.

When the show ends, I'm still feeling bummed out that my interaction with Brandon—someone I never thought I'd see again—only lasted for a few minutes. Lacey finds me at the bar, and we head out behind the other concertgoers.

When we reach the top step, Brandon suddenly reappears, a grin on his face. "Where are you going?"

"Home," I say, heart thundering. "Why?"

"I thought maybe you wanted to get a bite to eat or something."

Lacey nudges me with her elbow. "Go ahead, go. I can grab a cab back to campus."

"Campus?" He raises an eyebrow. "You're a schoolgirl?"

Lacey heads over to a bank of taxis parked nearby as Brandon grabs my hand. He walks me over to an old pick-up truck and opens the passenger door.

I climb in. "Wow. This is a cool old truck. Have you had it long?"

Brandon walks around the truck and slides behind the wheel. "It was my father's when he was young. He left it to me when he died." He starts the truck and pulls out onto the road.

"I'm sorry. It's terrible that you lost your father."

He shrugs. "Don't worry about it. It was a long time ago."

We pull up to a small mom-and-pop diner and go inside. A half a dozen booths sit against one side of the paint-peeled walls. As soon as we sit down, the waitress walks over and drops two menus in front of us, then walks away without a word.

"Don't you want to know what we'd like to drink?" Brandon calls after her.

The woman turns around, looking unimpressed, and slowly makes her way back to the table.

"I'll have a large Coke, and my beautiful friend here will have..." He looks at me. "What will you have?"

"A soda water with lime, please," I say to the waitress.

As soon as she walks away, we start to laugh. "She's probably not known for having great people skills," Brandon says.

The light in the diner is dim with a blue hue, which normally makes people look sallow and sickly, but not him. Brandon looks even more stunning now that he's sitting directly across from me. Thankfully I have the menu to hide behind. I'm afraid he'll find some horrible flaw if he looks at me for too long.

The waitress returns with our drinks, and we both order a burger and fries.

I watch the waitress amble away. "This place is pretty shabby. I hope the food is safe."

Brandon laughs. "It's a run-down joint, but the food is great." He takes a long sip of his drink. "So, tell me, Sophie-the-school girl, do you have family here?"

I shake my head. "Nope. It's just me. My parents are living abroad. What about you? Any family nearby?"

"Nope. The closest family I have is in Toronto—my mom."

"And you're here all alone?"

He smiles. "I have a few buddies around town, and a cousin. Other than them, yeah, I'm alone."

I smile. "Just like me."

For the next couple of hours, we talk about everything. He tells me what he does for a living—restores old cars—and we talk about me and school. Somewhere in the time we're chatting, I get confident enough to lift my eyes to meet his. And even though I'm still intimidated by his unmatchable good looks, I'm more focussed on what he's saying.

He tells me that his mom got remarried, and that he can't stand her new husband. Apparently the guy is a drinker and abused him when he was younger. When I ask him why his mother is with someone like that, he tells me that she drinks, too. In his eyes, I can see what a gentle and beautiful person he is, and I feel terrible that he had to endure what he did growing up.

We continue talking until the not-so-friendly waitress comes back, puts the bill on the table, and tells us it's closing time. When I glance at my watch, I can't believe it's 1AM. It felt like no time at all.

Brandon pays for our food, and even though the waitress was as cold as a block of ice, he leaves her a nice tip.

On the drive back to my car, he reaches over and touches my hand. "What are you doing tomorrow?"

"I don't know. Probably just getting ready for classes."

"That's great that you're serious about your studies. Maybe you'll come away with a degree and you won't end up doing grunt work, like I do."

"There's nothing wrong with working on cars, Brandon, if it's what you like to do."

"It's okay for now, but I've got bigger plans for my future."

I'm just about to ask him about his long-term goals when we pull up alongside my car. He reaches across me and opens the glove box to pull out a pen. Then he takes my hand in his and kisses it before writing his number on the side of my thumb. "Maybe when you're done studying, you can call me and we'll hang out some more." His voice is sweet and he sounds a little vulnerable.

Brandon gets out of the truck and holds the door open for me, then waits until I'm safely in my car before driving away.

As I pull out of the club lot and turn onto South Fraser Way, I can't contain myself. I scream at the windshield, "Oh my gosh. What just happened? I can't believe someone as incredible as him just spent the whole evening with me. And now he wants to see me again? This is crazy!"

I never focus on my looks. Ever. But for the first time in forever—maybe ever—I feel attractive and special.

Back in my unit, I am just about to wash my face when I remember Brandon's number on my hand. I grab a pen and paper and jot the number down, then place it safely on my dresser.

* * *

At the end of the professor's lecture, it occurs to me that I haven't heard a thing she said. During my next class, the words on the page of the textbook blend into each other as I strain to focus.

All I can think about is Brandon. It's taken all of my willpower not to call him. I don't want him to think I'm too eager, like a schoolgirl with a crush.

Pushing against the cold, powerful wind, I make my way across the campus. By the time I'm in my unit, my hands and face feel like ice. I quickly put the kettle on for tea, then get changed into my ugly sweats.

While looking for a warm shirt in my dresser, I notice Brandon's number sitting beside the lamp. I want to call him, but I'm scared.

What if, over the past few days, he found another girl to hang with? A girl that's more attractive than me? Or what if, when I call and he picks up the phone, he doesn't want to speak to me? The awkward silence would be too much to bear.

I forgo making the call and lie down on my bed. I try to distract myself by going over what I have to do for homework, but it doesn't last long; after a few minutes, I'm back to thinking about Brandon.

Screw it. I'm never going to relax unless I do it.

I take a deep breath and muster as much fake bravery as I can, then punch the number into my phone. As soon as it rings, my anxiety heightens and I want to hang up.

The phone clicks on the second ring, and his warm voice comes through. "Hello?"

"Hey." My voice is high, and I try to calm down. "How are you? I just thought I'd call and say thanks for dinner the other night."

"Is that really why you called?" His tone is amused.

"Um, yeah. And...I guess I wanted to say hi."

Brandon laughs. "I thought maybe you had such a good time with me that you were calling to see if I wanted to get together again."

I giggle like an idiot. "Of course. I mean, I guess so."

Shut up, Sophie! You sound like a blithering fool.

"Can I ask you a question?" he says.

"Yeah?"

"Who is this?"

My heart drops. Is he serious? Oh no. I want to hang up, put my pillow over my head, and scream.

"I'm just kidding, Sophie. Of course I know who you are."

I sigh with relief. "That was horrible of you. Jerk."

"I'm sorry."

We talk about his work at the shop for a while. Then he asks me how things are going at school. After a half hour or so, he tells me that he has to return a call from his boss, but he'd love to see me tomorrow night, if I'm available.

By the time I get off the phone, I'm grinning from ear to ear. I feel light and euphoric.

For the rest of the evening, I can't do anything but think about seeing Brandon tomorrow.

* * *

Dark clouds churn overhead as I make my way from my last class to my unit. I hope it doesn't rain—I don't want any reason for Brandon to cancel our date.

I have a shower, then spend a lot of time doing my hair and putting on just the right amount of makeup. I'm not sure what to wear, as he didn't tell me where we'd be going, so I opt for a pair of blue jeans, a white button-up shirt, and a wrap-around sweater.

After I'm dressed, I walk past the mirror and frown at my reflection. Tessa was right. I do dress frumpy.

I quickly switch the sweater for my old jean jacket. I'm probably going to freeze, but at least I won't look like someone's grandma.

Brandon calls just as I'm putting my shoes on. "Meet me downstairs at the entrance," he tells me.

He looks freshly showered and GQ, with his dark hair styled and his clothes fitted to his toned physique. As soon as I hop into his truck, my anxiety returns and I can feel my palms begin to sweat.

He smiles. "You look great."

"Really? I mean, thank you."

I ask where we're going, and he tells me there's an old movie playing at High Street Mall that he's been wanting to see. "It's called Young Frankenstein. It's a black-and-white comedy. Are you okay with that?"

"Of course, I love old movies," I lie.

The only time I think I've ever sat through a black-and-white movie is when my grandparents were still alive and they visited us from Scotland. My parents made me sit there with them as they watched the most boring shows I'd ever seen.

Still, I'm not the least bit put-off. As long as I get to be with Brandon, I'd sit in a room and stare at blank walls.

He pays for our tickets, and we get popcorn and drinks. When we walk inside, he leads me to the very back row of seats.

I sit down. "Wow. Are you sure we'll be able to see the screen from way back here?"

"Yeah. You'll see when the movie starts. I can't stand sitting at the front. There are always people pushing past you to get to their seats. Back here, we can stretch out a bit and not get bothered."

Halfway through the movie, we're laughing so hard, we can barely finish the popcorn. By the ending, my stomach muscles hurt and whatever mascara I had on has rolled down my cheeks.

Back in the truck, Brandon looks at me with a grin. "Where should we go now?"

I look at my watch. It's 11PM and my first class is super early tomorrow. "It doesn't matter to me. Where do you feel like going?"

"We could go for a drive. I know this cool spot by the river, if you're into it."

"Yeah. For sure. I don't have to be anywhere."

"Are you sure? It's getting late, and you probably have school in the morning."

"Nah," I lie. "I don't have any classes until the afternoon."

Brandon drives to Sumas Highway and takes the bridge into Mission. As he drives,

I notice a sign that says Deroche, 22 kilometers.

Driving down the winding road, Brandon slips a CD in the stereo. Much to my surprise, Van Morrison starts to play. Judging by his age and looks, I would've expected Brandon to play something more contemporary. I'm completely into old rock, so this is just one more thing I can add to the list of what makes him so cool.

It isn't long before we arrive, and as soon as Brandon turns the truck off, I can hear the sound of the rushing river. We jump out of the truck and he takes my hand.

He walks me a few feet down a narrow path that winds around tall Hemlock and Red Cedar trees. When we reach the riverbank, he leads me to a flat rock and we sit side by side. I look up through the treetops and am transfixed by the millions of stars in the night sky.

Just then, a surge of water crashes over a large smooth stone and sprays us. I squeal and lean back. "You knew that was going to happen if we sat here," I accuse him.

Brandon laughs and apologizes.

After twenty minutes or so, it starts to get a bit too cool, so we walk back and sit in the truck. Brandon turns on the heat to warm us up and is just about to put music on when I stop him. "No. I'd rather talk and get to know you better. If that's okay."

He smiles. "No problem. What do you want to know?"

I shrug. "I guess everything you want to tell me."

"I'm pretty boring. If I start talking about myself, you may fall asleep."

"It's a risk I'm willing to take. So, do you have a lot of friends?"

He shakes his head. "Nope. I'm a hermit, much like you. I have a lot of acquaintances because of my job. Otherwise, I usually only hang with my roomies."

I nod. "Are they from back East, or did you meet them here?"

"I met them here. Their names are Ryder and Sylvie. They're a couple."

I think about what I can ask him, but considering he's a self-proclaimed hermit, he probably has a boring life, much like me.

"How about you, Miss Sophie? Do you have any deep dark secrets?"

"Yeah, right. My life is pretty linear and predictable so far."

"And then you met me." He winks.

"What about you? Any deep dark secrets?"

He thinks for a minute, then looks away and fumbles with the steering wheel. "I guess I have one, but I don't want to tell you in case you think less of me. Then again, I like you, and I think it's important to start off a friendship with complete honesty."

I pat his leg. "Don't worry. I'm not the judgemental type."

He takes a deep breath, then rolls up his sleeve. There's a small tattoo on his bicep that says CB9-512.

"What does that mean?"

"Cellblock nine, inmate five-twelve."

Taken aback, I fight to find my words. "Jail? You were in jail?"

Brandon pulls his sleeve back down, covering the tattoo. "Maybe I shouldn't have shown you that."

"No. Of course you should have. I'm sorry if I paused. I just haven't met anyone who was in jail before."

"Well, before you assume the worst, I'll tell you what happened. It was when I first moved to BC. My cousin, who could almost pass as my twin, invited me to live with him until I got on my feet. So I made the biggest mistake of my life and took him up on his offer."

"Oh no. He got you into crime?"

"He tried to, but it wasn't my thing. Anyway, I started to see a lot of things come into this apartment that I knew must be stolen. Then, he started getting into drugs. I couldn't find a job and had limited money, so I was kind of stuck staying with him."

"That's terrible. Did he eventually get straight?"

"Yeah, he did a few months in jail after getting busted a few times. But when he got out, he was really motivated to change his life. He quit the dope and met a nice girl. A while later, she got pregnant. That's when my cousin got hired at the car detail shop and got me in, too."

"That's great."

"It was, for a while. Until he got into a fight with his girlfriend and relapsed. He came home stoned out of his head with a car full of stolen goods. Not long after, the cops raided our place."

"Oh no. And his poor girlfriend was pregnant at the time. Talk about a bad decision. He basically threw his life away."

"No. He didn't."

"What do you mean?"

Brandon sighs. "I took the rap for him."

"You what?"

"Yeah. I couldn't see him go to jail. Not with a kid on the way."

"That's crazy. And the cops believed you?"

"Yeah. They didn't look too hard into it. They just wanted the file closed. Plus, my cousin and I looked a lot alike, and the eyewitness they had couldn't rule me out as the suspect."

"Wow. What a huge gift you gave. How much time did you do?"

"Six months."

I shake my head. "And now you have a criminal record for something you didn't do?"

"Pretty much." He looks somber for a few moments, then suddenly snaps out of it, smiling at me. "There you have it. You know all of my dark secrets."

What a wonderful person he is. I can't believe he sacrificed his freedom for his messed-up cousin. I tell him this, but he just shrugs it off. "I did what I thought was right at the time."

"But weren't you scared while you were in jail?"

Brandon nods. "Yeah. I was pretty scrawny back then. That's why I started working out, to protect myself."

"You've had quite a history."

"Anyways, enough about me. It's your turn to shock me."

I laugh. "The only shock is going to be how dull my life has been."

He smirks. "Oh, come on. I'm sure there's some drama in there somewhere."

"Nope. Nothing thrilling at all. I lived with my mom and dad until recently when they moved back to Scotland. Other than helping my father in his hardware store, I've never had a job on my own. I live on campus and I study. That's about it."

"Wow. You were right. You are super dull."

I poke him. "You jerk."

Before I know it, he's tickling me and I'm trying to tickle him back. When we finally stop to catch our breath, he leans in close, looks into my eyes, then slowly kisses me. His lips are soft and moist and his breath is warm and sweet.

This is the first time I've kissed anyone except the guy I dated for two years in high school—Shayne. He was about as interesting as a stick and had a personality to match. Of course, my parents loved him and were devastated when we broke up. They thought he was safe and reliable, two qualities that old people look for when buying a car. I was always far more interested in guys that were unpredictable and a bit wild. But working for my parents for the past three years made it so I couldn't pursue dating, especially since I was still living at home. They were old school, with a religious twist.

Our kisses soon spawn heavy petting, and it isn't long before the windows are fogging up. My heart is pounding inside my chest and my whole body feels electrified. I run my hands over his biceps and across his muscular chest. He stops kissing my lips and focuses on my neck, running his tongue gently over my skin.

My body tenses in response and my breathing quickens to the point of panting. I want him so badly, I can't stand it. He presses his chest against mine and by the thumping of his heart, I know he wants me, too.

Slowly he removes his top, and the reflection of the dash lights shine on his perfectly sculpted body.

"You're incredible," I whisper, not meaning to say it out loud.

He starts undoing my shirt. "So are you."

My chest heaves as, one by one, he opens each button until my lace bra is exposed. He looks down at my chest and smiles. "You're beautiful."

I can't believe I'm here right now with this perfect creature, and to know he wants me as much as I want him.

When he reaches around and starts manipulating the clasp on my bra, a bright flash of light shines in through the back window. I immediately slouch down and, as fast as I can, do up the buttons on my shirt. Brandon sits up straight and slides his top on. The light illuminates the inside of the truck for a few more moments before it finally shifts and starts to fade. Brandon looks in the rear-view window and shakes his head. "It's not the cops. It's just some car parking."

Sure enough, the vehicle pulls up beside us. When I look out of the window, I see a couple, both around twenty, looking back.

I start to laugh. "This must be a popular place for people to come and make out."

Brandon giggles. "Maybe it is. I just wanted to show you the river and talk a while, but I kind of lost control."

"Me too." I smile, straightening out my shirt.

"Do you think we should go?"

"Yeah. Probably." My pulse rate is returning to normal.

On the drive back to Abbotsford, he motions for me to sit close to him. When he's not shifting gears, his hand is resting on my knee.

* * *

My eyes wander up and down the textured white ceiling as my thoughts drift around the room. Even though my head rests on my pillow, I feel like I'm floating above my bed—I'm in a complete state of euphoria as images of my perfect evening with Brandon replay in my mind.

In retrospect, I'm glad the car pulled up next to us when it did. Even though I had lost most of my self-control in the heat of the moment, I can see now that having sex with him so soon in our relationship could've been a mistake. Besides, when we see one another again, we'll still have that sexual tension between us that you only get once, right at the very beginning.

I hated having sex with Shayne, my ex. His idea of passion was waiting for my parents to be away, then planning the evening to a tee——down to where we would have sex in the house, and what underwear he was going to wear for the grand event. And the actual act was even more predictable and dull. We'd take our clothes off, usually in my room. Then he'd climb on top of me, kiss me with a hard, closed mouth, then enter me as I looked around my bedroom, studying my track and field trophies and my teddy bear collection in the corner. I think the only reason I did it was because I felt the only thing more pathetic than having sex with someone you had zero attraction to was still being a virgin in my senior year of high school.

The annoying ring of the phone pierces my ears and wakes me from a deep sleep. I look over at the clock and see that it's 2:30 in the morning. *Who would be calling me now?*

Then I think of my parents, and how it's 10:30 in the morning there. My mom and dad know the time difference between us, so they wouldn't call me at this hour unless something was wrong. I quickly sit up, reach over to the nightstand, and answer the phone.

"Hello?" My voice is weak and groggy.

"Sophie?" a broken voice says back.

I can tell right away it's not either of my parents, so I look down at the receiver and see a number I don't recognize. "Who is this?"

The female voice starts to cry, then cuts out.

"Hello? Who's calling?"

"It's me. Tessa."

"Tessa? It doesn't sound like you. What's wrong?"

She strains to gain control. "I…I'm in really big trouble and I have nowhere to go. Can I come to your unit?"

"Um…It's super late, but yeah. If you have no place else you can go."

I barely get my robe on and make it to the front room before there's a knock at the door. *That was fast. She must've been in front of the building, knowing I wouldn't turn her away.*

If I hadn't known her since childhood, I would never have recognized her when I opened the door. She's wearing a mac jacket that's miles too big for her and smells of gasoline. Her hair is greasy and stuck to the sides of her face, and her eyes have the same dark circles they did the last time I saw her.

As soon as our eyes meet, she starts to sob, then lunges into my arms. I've never seen her this emotional before. Turning my head to avoid the pungent odor of petrol, I gently pat her back, then walk her over to the sofa to sit down. I hand her a box of Kleenex, then get up and put the kettle on for tea.

"Things couldn't be much worse, Sophie. I didn't know where else to go."

Once the water is boiled, I fill the teapot, then join her on the sofa. She wipes her raccoon eyes and looks at me. "I can't believe how stupid I am."

"What's happened, Tess?"

"I got so stoned, I couldn't remember if I took my pill."

"You were doing drugs? Really?"

Tessa nods. "Yeah. And I know what your opinion is on drugs, but I really don't need a lecture right now."

I take a deep breath. "And what pill did you forget to take?"

"My birth control pill."

Her answer stops me in my tracks.

"And now I'm knocked up."

"Wait. Just slow down for a minute. How long ago was it that you forgot to take the pill?"

"Weeks ago," she sobs. "And then, when I didn't get my period, I just knew I was pregnant."

I sit back against the sofa and take a deep breath, trying to process the information.

"I told my so-called boyfriend, and instead of being supportive, he said he never wants to see me again. We were in

Hope at the time, and I had no way to get back to Abbotsford."

"What a complete jerk! What did you do then?"

"Luckily we were at a truck-stop diner, so I went inside and asked if anyone was headed West. Finally, an older guy said he'd give me a ride. He let me off on the side of McCallum Road and I walked the rest of the way here."

I put my hand on her shoulder. "Don't worry, Tess. It's going to be okay. Drink your tea and get some sleep. It'll be easier to think of a plan in the morning."

She leans into me. "Thanks, Sophie. I've been feeling so alone."

"Well, you're not alone. You've got me."

Chapter Four

My eyes open to the melodic songs of small birds as they fly past my window. I know I have classes in a while, but I stay in bed, thinking about Tessa's situation.

She's the most irresponsible girl I've ever met. My parents used to refer to her as the whirling dervish because she was always so scattered and never could stick to anything she started.

I feel sorry for her, in the predicament she's in. If anything, this will be a good wake-up call and she'll have no choice but to start being more responsible. I think about her parents and the looks on their faces when she tells them she's pregnant. No doubt, she'll make me go along with her.

I glance at the clock and decide that I'd better get out of bed and get dressed. Then I should make Tessa some breakfast. She's so thin and gaunt, she probably hasn't eaten in a long time.

Once I'm dressed, I open my bedroom door and walk into the front room. Tessa's bedroom door is open, and the bed is empty. Then, I notice a piece of paper on her pillow.

In Tessa's messy writing, it says:

Sophie. Thank you for taking me in. You're a beautiful person. I had to leave quickly, but I'll be back. I'll explain later.

I shake my head. Yep, the whirling dervish.

* * *

It's late in the afternoon and I'm finally back in my unit after my classes when my cell rings. No doubt it's Tessa, asking to come back. When I pick up my phone, I smile when I see Brandon's number on the display.

"Hello, beautiful."

"Hi, Brandon. How are you?"

"I'm great now that I'm talking to you. Did you have a good night?"

"I did, until I came home."

He laughs. "Yeah, I had fun with you, too. After that, I had to come home and have a cool shower."

We laugh.

"So, did you go to bed early or were you hitting the books?"

"I did a bit of reading, not much." I let out a giggle. "For some reason, I couldn't keep my mind on my homework."

I want to tell him about Tessa and how I was up half the night with her, but I stop myself. It's not my news to tell.

"Are you busy later?" he asks.

"I don't have anything much going on. Why? Do you have something in mind?"

"I was thinking of maybe coming over to your place and making you dinner."

I look over at my microwave, then at the toaster. "My unit doesn't have an oven in it. There's a common area for cooking. Maybe I should come to your place?"

"I'd love to have you over, but I'm living in a tiny room above the shop and there's definitely nothing here to cook with."

After shooting ideas back and forth for a while, we agree that Brandon will pick up a frozen lasagna and cook it in my microwave.

I spend the next hour and a half cleaning up my place before having a shower and doing my hair and make-up. I'm nervous about him coming over and I'm not sure why.

There's a huge part of me that hopes a few residents see Brandon coming to my door. If that happened, it would definitely turn a few heads and spark some funny gossip about me. Up to now, I've always been viewed as the anti-social girl in unit #5. I've never had company, other than my parents when I first moved in.

* * *

I put on some music—"The Last Waltz" by The Band—and turn the volume low enough to talk over. Brandon knocks on the door just as I'm putting my textbooks off to the side.

He looks as he always does. Amazingly hot. His hair is freshly styled and he's wearing tight blue jeans and a form-fitted white t-shirt. He's brought with him a bottle of wine and the frozen lasagna.

With the door to the hallway still open, I take the food and invite him in. I smile when I see two girls walking past and glaring at Brandon, then at me.

"Wow. This place was hard to find," he says.

"Did you get lost?"

"For a few minutes, yes. Then, I just followed the smart-looking people and I finally found you."

I laugh as I get two glasses from the cupboard.

Brandon pours the wine and I put the lasagna in the microwave. We sit together on the sofa and sip our wine.

He smiles at me. "Thanks for having me over."

I'm getting braver around him now. I look him in the eyes and tell him I'm glad he's here.

When "The Weight" starts to play, he sets his glass down, then takes mine and puts it beside his. He stands up and reaches out his hand to me.

I smile. "What?"

"Dance with me."

Instantly horrified, I shake my head. "Thanks, but I don't dance. I have two left feet."

He doesn't answer. He just keeps his hand out.

"Seriously, Brandon. You don't get it. I'm the type of person that falls going up the stairs. You don't want to risk it."

When he doesn't flinch, I know he's not going to let me off the hook. I shake my head, then grab his hand.

At first, there's a space between us and I'm fumbling to do something with my legs. Then, he pulls me tightly into him and slowly starts to move. I can feel his hips gyrating against mine. His body is relaxed and his moves are fluid and making me tingle everywhere.

Following his lead, I manage not to step on his feet as he moves me across the small room.

"Kiss me," he whispers.

As he lowers his lips to meet mine, I raise onto my tiptoes. Just as our mouths touch, there's a loud bang on the door.

This can't be happening.

I tell him not to move, then walk to the door and open it.

Tessa is standing in front of me, holding bags full of chips and other junk food. "Hey, Sophie. Sorry I didn't call first, but my cell died."

I give her a strained look and wink, hoping she catches on that I'm not alone.

"What?" She looks confused. "Is there something in your eye?"

I quickly shake my head.

"You're acting weird."

I slowly shift over so she can see Brandon standing in the living room behind me.

She looks at him, then at me with disbelief. "Oh, wow. You have company?"

"I do. Yes." I hope she gets the message that now isn't a good time for her to be here.

She grins. "Oh wow. Is that the same guy from Cultus Lake?"

I lean forward. "Yes. It is," I whisper. "Can you come back later?"

"Yeah, I guess I could walk around or go for a coffee somewhere. But first I need to put these groceries away."

I hold out my arms to indicate that I'll take the bags for her, but she ignores me and barges past. I turn to see Brandon still standing where I left him and looking confused. I close the door. "Brandon, this is Tessa."

"Hey, Brandon," Tess says. "Sorry if I'm interrupting. I'll only be a minute, then I'll be out of here."

"No problem." He walks over and sits on the sofa.

I quickly turn the music off.

"Man, I tell ya." Tess packs her junk food in the cupboard. "I've been out for hours, walking around stores and trying to distract myself from everything that's going on."

I grin. "You'll have to tell me all about it—later."

Tess walks past the microwave. "Ooh. Are you cooking Italian? It smells amazing. I'm completely starving."

"Brandon brought it over for him and me," I say, dropping another hint that she should leave.

"Well, if you're hungry, there's more than enough for you to have some, too," Brandon says.

And right then, I knew that our evening together was ruined before it started.

"Oh, I don't want to impose," Tess says.

Sure, you do. Otherwise, you would have left instead of talking and procrastinating.

"I love Italian food," Tess continues. "I'd love to stay as long as it's okay with you, Sophie."

I force a fake grin. "Why not."

Tessa sets the table. When the microwave beeps, I put the food on the table, along with plates and utensils. The three of us chit-chat about nothing much while we eat. Inside, I can't help resenting Tessa a little. She knew exactly what she was doing when she wormed her way into Brandon's and my evening. Now, every hope I had of having a nice intimate evening with him is gone.

As the meal progresses, Tessa blabs about literally everything—her ex-trucker boyfriend, parties she went to on the road, and the new drugs she was recently introduced to. Neither Brandon nor I have been able to get a word in edgewise, so we resign ourselves to nodding and smiling.

It feels like eternity for dinner to be over, though we've only been at the table for an hour. Tessa finishes her lasagna and, after leaving her dirty plate and cutlery, goes to the sofa to flop out and watch TV.

Brandon helps me clear the table, then he and I go to my room. He shuts the door behind him, then turns and grins at me. "Well, that was different."

I give an apologetic shrug. "I know. I'm so sorry about that. She just kind of goes on and on without giving much thought to anyone else.".

I sit on the edge of the bed and Brandon sits beside me. "Don't worry about it. We couldn't let her go hungry, so we did the right thing. But yeah, there was one point where she was talking so much and so fast, I thought I saw smoke coming from her lips."

I laugh a bit too loudly and cover my mouth. I wouldn't want Tessa to hear us and get hurt feelings.

Just as we start talking and get comfortable on my bed, Tessa turns the TV up annoyingly loud. It becomes obvious that she's trying to keep Brandon and me from enjoying any alone time.

Brandon shakes his head. "Well, we've got two choices. We can end the evening and say good night, or I can take you out for ice cream."

I smile. "I really don't want to end the night yet."

He hops off the bed. "Ice cream it is!"

I tell Tessa that I'll be back in a while. She looks genuinely disappointed that she couldn't succeed in ruining Brandon's and my time together. She's jealous that I have someone right now, and she doesn't.

* * *

The neon lights above the building buzz and crackle as we walk into Dairy Queen. Brandon orders us each a cone, then we walk outside and sit on the patio. We sit close to avoid yelling over the sound of traffic on Sumas Highway.

"I'm sorry we were interrupted at my place. I'm sure it would've been a lot more convenient to talk there."

Brandon smiles. "Nah. This is fine. Anywhere I am with you is fun."

I feel my face blush. "I feel the same way."

"Though, I must admit, your roomie Tess is a bit...interesting."

"She's actually not my roommate anymore. She just needs a place to crash temporarily."

"Temporarily?"

I nod. "I don't expect she'll be there long. She's never anywhere for very long."

"Well, then, I guess we have something to look forward to."

"It must be hard for you, living above a workshop. Is it noisy?"

"It can be. Mostly I'm frustrated by all the people coming and going. I'm private, and once I hang up my coveralls for the day, I like to retire to a quiet place to unwind."

"How long will it be before you get your own place?"

"Actually, I'm just waiting for my buddy Ryder and his girlfriend Sylvie to find us a place. Somewhere with an upstairs and a downstairs, so I can live in one half of the house and they can live in the other."

I nod, and am just taking the last bite of my cone when a homeless man pushing a cart wheels up. "Hey, folks, you got any money?"

I look at Brandon and predict he'll tell the man to go away. But instead, he stands up, reaches into his pocket, and pulls out his wallet. He tugs out a twenty-dollar bill and hands it to the man. "Here you go, brother. Get yourself something to eat."

The man's expression is one of gratitude and relief. He thanks Brandon, smiles a toothless grin, then slowly ambles away.

I'm staring at Brandon in wonder. "That was really cool of you to help that man out."

"Well, the way I see it is, most people live paycheck to paycheck and sometimes life can throw a curveball. I'm sure, at some point, that man had a family and a job, and something happened to derail his life. I guess what I'm trying to say is, I never take anything for granted because things can change fast and you never know what the future holds. That's why I try not to judge."

I smile. "I've never met anyone like you before. It's like you're a wise old man, living in a young man's body."

Brandon laughs. "Thanks, but you give me too much credit. I just try to stay humble, keep my head down, and march through life like everyone else."

On the ride back to campus, I'm filled with warmth and respect for my new friend. Meeting someone as special as him, I don't know how I got so lucky. I just hope I can spend more time getting to know him.

After a few minutes spent on a long, passionate kiss in front of my place, I thank him for the wonderful evening and get out of the truck. As I walk to the entrance of the building, I look back and see him watching to make sure I get inside safely.

* * *

An acrid odor wafts up the corridor and intensifies the closer I get to my unit. I open the door and see Tessa trying to blow smoke out the small opening in the window.

I close the door hard. "You're not allowed to smoke in here. I'm sure you remember that in the rule book when we moved in."

She attempts to wave the smoke out the window, but it's pointless. The entire room smells like an ashtray.

"Tessa, put it out! Besides, you shouldn't be smoking if you're pregnant."

"Actually, I've decided to get an abortion, so it doesn't really matter."

Not knowing how to answer, I go to my room. I know her well enough to see that she's trying to change the subject by shocking me. I'm already pissed at her for ruining what was supposed to be an intimate dinner with Brandon. Now, she's putting me at risk of getting tossed out of my place because she's decided to go against the strict rules. I wish I hadn't agreed to let her stay here. I can't help but wonder about whatever bullshit scheme she's going to pull next.

I lie on my bed and seethe about how disrespected I feel. Then, after a while, I decide not to give Tess any more of my energy, and I start thinking about the one person who makes me happy.

I can't wait to see him again. Maybe by the next time we make dinner plans, Tessa will have found a place to stay, and Brandon and I can finish that dance. Then we can follow where our passion takes us.

I haven't known Brandon long enough to consider having sex, but I can't help it. He's perfect in every way, and I desire him. It's not just because of his unmatchable great looks, it's something more than that. I see such a kindred spirit in him that I can't get enough of. It's baffling how he's still single. I guess he's like I am—cautious and picky.

I'm just dozing off when Tessa raps hard on my door. Then, without waiting for me to respond, she opens it. "Sophie, can I talk to you for a moment?"

"I'm tired, Tessa. Can we talk tomorrow?"

"It kind of can't wait."

Frustrated and not wanting to hear anything she has to say, I sit up and stare at her, hoping whatever she has to say is brief.

"You look upset with me. I know I blew your evening, and I wanted to apologize. I guess I just panicked."

"Panicked?" My tone is cold.

"Yes. I saw Brandon here and right away I was afraid you would get into a relationship with him and forget about me. You're my only friend, Soph, and I really need you right now."

I shake my head. "Nice try. I'm not your only friend. You're a social butterfly. I'm just the only person you know that will let you stay with them."

"That's not true! I have a lot of acquaintances, yes, but that's different than having someone you trust and can confide in. Think about it, Sophie. Our parents were in business together for years. We've known each other for years. Doesn't that count for something?"

"Yes. I just think you need to consider how your actions affect other people sometimes."

Surprisingly, she doesn't try to defend herself further. She just nods. "You really like this guy, huh?"

"I do. It all still feels pretty surreal. I mean, who would've ever thought I could get a guy as hot or as wonderful as Brandon?"

Tessa tilts her head in confusion. "Are you kidding me? You're beautiful, Sophie. The only one that doesn't know that is you. Granted, you do dress like a frugal grandmother sometimes, and you should seriously rethink some of your drab hairdos, but you're a stunning girl."

I laugh at the criticisms she threw in with her compliments. "I don't think I'm anything special. But thanks."

Tessa shakes her head. "Do you know what your problem is?"

"I have shitty taste in roommates?"

"Very funny. No. Your problem is that you have no idea how to be a girl. Other than knowing how to dress like my grandma, of course."

I take one of my pillows off the bed and pelt her with it. Right away, she grabs the other one and wacks me back. Soon, we're in a full-fledged pillow fight. By the time it finally ends, we're laughing so hard we can no longer hurl the pillows around. We both flop out on the bed, facing each other.

"You know what I think you need?" Tessa says.

"For you to not be here the next time Brandon comes over?"

"Ok. Yes. I agree with that. But also, I think you need to come shopping with me tomorrow and buy some fun, new clothes and makeup."

I scoff. "With what money? I'm on a tight budget, especially now that my parents retired and I don't work for them anymore."

"Speaking of your parents, have you told them about Brandon yet?"

My eyes widen. "Are you mad? My father would lose his head if he knew I was with some guy I just met. You don't know how strict they were about boys when I was growing up."

"But they let you date Shayne in high school."

"That's because he wasn't a threat. He was like Steve Urkel crossed with Pee Wee Herman—any parent would love their daughter to date someone as non-threatening as him."

Tessa smiles. "Yeah, I remember seeing him come into the shop when you two were together. I thought you were polar opposites."

"True, but I've seen some of the winners you hung out with. I think I'd rather have Shayne."

"It doesn't matter now. Those days are long behind us. So, what do you think? Should we take the day tomorrow to get you dolled up, then maybe grab a bite to eat somewhere? I promise, we'll only go to the cheaper stores."

I hum and haw for a few moments. "I don't know."

"Come on, Soph. Don't you want to look good for your hot new boyfriend?"

"He's not my boyfriend. But okay. I guess I'll trust you and let you take me shopping."

Tessa gets up from the bed and walks to the door, then turns to me. "I'm glad I'm here with you. And thanks for putting up with me. I'm really thinking a lot about getting my shit together. I think I'm going to talk to admin sometime next week and see about getting back into school." For the first time since I've known her, she looks serious and focused.

"I think that would be a great idea, girl. You've got a lot of potential. I'm super proud of you for thinking about taking that step."

"Night, Soph." She shuts the door behind her.

Chapter Five

A powerful gust of cool wind rushes through the small opening of my window and sends a chill over my bare skin. I open my eyes and look out at the angry, dark morning.

I get up and grab my housecoat from the hook on the back of my bedroom door. Once the warm fleece is against my body, I walk into the front room.

Tess is gone, but all her belongings are still here. The time on the microwave says 10AM. It's way too early for Tess to be up and already out of the suite.

Baffled, I go to put grounds in the coffee maker when I notice a note on the counter from Tessa.

It's 2AM and I can't sleep. I'm just going to walk down to the 7/11 and grab a bag of chips, and I'll be right back. Just thought I'd leave a note in case you got up for a glass of water and saw that I wasn't here.

I had a great talk with you last night. Hopefully, we can do more of that now that I'm getting my shit together. XO Tess

She left the unit over eight hours ago.

While the coffee percolates, I tell myself that maybe she went next door to visit with one of the students she's familiar with. Or maybe she's in the laundry room down the hall.

I forgo my morning cup of java and quickly put on my ugly sweats and slippers. As soon as I open my front door, two girls who live on the floor walk by. I ask them both if they've seen Tessa, but neither have. I hurry down to the laundry room, but the machines are empty and there's no one around. *Where the hell is she?*

Back in my unit, I go through the garbage, looking for anything new, but all I find is the empty lasagne container and the junk food wrappers from last night. I grab my cell and check for new messages, but there aren't any. I quickly text Tessa to call me.

Leaving in the middle of the night is something not out of character for her, but after last night and how she seemed so driven to change her ways, I'm shocked that she would just up and split. And then there's the note. If she was taking off to meet some guy, she definitely wouldn't bother to leave me a note, especially one that said she was happy about getting her life back on track.

No. Something is definitely wrong here. I can feel it in the pit of my gut.

By noon, I'd thought of every possible scenario about what could've happened to Tessa, and none of them are good. The most probable scenario is that she went to the 7/11, as she'd written, then met some smooth-talking guy and went home with him. She's probably still sleeping in his bed right now.

I have things to pick up today—a parcel from my parents at the post office, toiletries from the grocery store, and bulk paper from Staples. I think about how excited Tessa was to take me shopping today. I can't believe I bought into her bullshit again. I bet she'll be all hungover and apologetic in a few hours when she bangs on my door. This time, I'm not going to listen when she spews off another lame reason why she, yet again, didn't keep her word. I'm done.

I dress in warm clothes to combat the ugly weather, then head out. As soon as I'm in the car and turn the key in the ignition, my cell rings. I smile when I see Brandon's number. It's a perfect distraction to take my mind off Tessa.

"Hi, Brandon. How's it going?"

"Better now that I have some time to talk to you. I've had quite the morning, I was woken up at 2AM by my boss. Had to rescue him from a bar because he was too pissed to drive home. I've really got to rethink my working and living situation. I'm far too accessible to him here."

"Wow. That's not good. He's very lucky to have you."

"Yeah, well. Jobs are scarce and I put up with a lot for the measly wage I get. But enough about me. Did you get a good sleep? What did you do today?"

I tell him about Tess and how she pulled another disappearing act on me. "At first I was worried, but after searching for her, it occurred to me that this could be just another of her stunts."

"You can't let her occupy space in your head. Not when she's being so inconsiderate of your time and feelings. You've got your own life to lead."

He's right. I shouldn't fall for her con jobs anymore. And letting her stay with me instead of having to make her own way is just enabling her. From now on, I'm going to say no.

"And there's another upside to you not letting her crash at your place anymore."

"Oh yeah? What's that?"

"You and I can spend some alone time together."

* * *

Day turns to night, and with no sign of Tessa, I decide to invite Brandon over. After having a shower, putting my hair in a ponytail, and getting dressed in a pair of tights and a T-shirt, I tidy up the unit and wait for Brandon.

It's almost 10PM before he shows up. His hair is freshly styled and he's wearing his usual attire of tight blue jeans and a t-shirt. I smile as he passes me a small bouquet of flowers.

"Thanks, Brandon. I love them."

He sits on the couch as I put the flowers in a vase and place them on the end table. As soon as I sit down next to him, he leans over and kisses me.

My skin shivers and small hairs rise on the back of my neck. With our lips pressed firmly together, Brandon slowly runs his hand under my shirt and starts to fondle my breasts. I, in turn, run my hand up his shirt and over his perfectly sculpted chest. As we touch one another, our breathing quickens, along with our heartbeats.

With every minute that passes, I can feel myself wanting him more and more. This time, there are no distractions to prevent us from going all the way.

He stands up, pulls his shirt over his head, and drops it on the sofa. He then leans over and pulls me into his arms.

As he carries me into the bedroom, his stunning eyes meet mine. "Are you okay? Are you sure you're ready?"

I nod slowly and smile, even though I'm a bit self-conscious about him seeing me naked. His body is perfect, and it's obvious he works hard to keep it that way, whereas the only exercise I get is on my short walks around campus.

Once he lays me on my bed, he slowly removes his jeans, not taking his eyes off me. I shuffle out of my tights and slip under the covers. He smiles and shakes his head, then pulls the blankets off me. "Don't hide. You're beautiful, and I want to see every inch of you."

From the bottom of the bed, he slowly crawls over me until we're face to face. As we start to kiss, he presses himself against me, and I can feel his excitement. He gently explores every curve of my body with his hands, causing the muscles in my body to contract.

Even though I've had sex before, this feels like the first time. With the rhythm of our heightened breathing and the cadence of our heartbeats, we melt into one and the world around us disappears. All that exists are him and me.

We make love until we're out of breath and exhausted. Brandon lies beside me and smiles, brushing the hair out of my face. "That was incredible."

"I feel the same way."

"I've been with a lot of girls before, but I can honestly say that I've never made love to any of them the way we just did. Being with you meant more to me than all of them combined."

I feel like I'm dreaming, because never in my life could I imagine having such a perfect guy fall for me. Then again, I never really gave any of them a chance, until now.

"Are you hungry?" I ask.

"Starved."

I wrap my housecoat around me, then go to the kitchen and make us a box of Kraft dinner in the hot pot. We sit cuddled up on the sofa and watch TV until the sun comes up.

Finally, Brandon looks at his watch and says that he has to be at work in a half hour.

"How are you going to work when you haven't slept yet?"

He winks. "With a big smile on my face."

* * *

The morning sun casts shadows on the wall. I rub my eyes and check the time on my phone. 5AM.

I couldn't doze off for hours after Brandon left yesterday morning. I felt too euphoric and excited to relax. It was only after we spoke on the phone when he was done with work that I finally started to get tired.

I lie in bed for another few minutes, looking out the window and wondering if

Brandon is awake and getting ready for work.

Just as I walk into the kitchen, my phone rings, and I have to go back into the bedroom to get it.

"Hello." My voice is raspy and quiet.

"Hi. Is Tessa there?"

Almost instantly I recognize the voice. It's Mrs. Waters, Tessa's mom.

I give her a brief rundown of the last time I saw her daughter, then tell her how she left me a note saying she'd be right back but hasn't returned since.

Tessa's mother sounds worried, even though they're well aware of their daughter's antics and how she's known for disappearing. "I'm just concerned because she was supposed to meet with her father and me a couple of days ago. She said she had something important to talk to us about, and she sounded serious this time."

All I could think was that Tess was going to tell them about her pregnancy, and how she desperately wanted to get back into university and change her life.

I do my best to reassure Mrs. Waters that Tessa was probably just at a friend's place and lost track of time. I then suggest she try to call Tessa.

"I have, repeatedly, but her phone goes right to voicemail each time. I'm starting to really worry."

I promise Mrs. Waters to pass the message on to Tess when I see her, and that I will call if I hear anything before then. When the call ends, I rack my brain once more, trying to think of where she could've gone. You'd think she would've reached out to me or her parents by now, especially in her condition.

I feel both mad at her for putting everyone through this again, but I also have a sudden worry that maybe something has made it so she can't call.

I spend the better part of the day doing laundry and editing some essays that are due tomorrow. It's after dinner when Brandon calls.

"How was your day, beautiful?"

I smile, flashing back to our passionate night. "It was okay. Nothing really exciting happened, apart from Tessa's mom calling."

"Oh? Did she finally turn up?"

I sigh. "Oddly enough, no. Usually, she would be in touch with her parents because she always ran out of cash and needs their help."

"I'm sure she'll turn up sooner or later. Though, it's kind of a shit move that she makes her parents worry."

"Yeah. I think so too. I just hope she's okay. I wasn't too worried until I heard her mother's voice on the phone. After that, it kind of had me worried, too."

"Don't worry your pretty little head about her. You should only be focussing your efforts on two things."

"What's that?"

"Your schoolwork, and us."

"I think I like focussing on us more than I do my homework."

"I was thinking about you all day, to the point of messing up at work."

I laugh in delight. "How did you mess up?"

"I was spray painting a car and started having flashbacks of making love to you. I accidentally screwed the wrong color paint onto the compressor."

"Oh no. Did you mess up the paint job?"

"No. Thankfully I caught my mistake before I started spraying."

We talk for almost three hours before Brandon tells me that he has another early morning at work tomorrow, and we say goodbye. After lying on the sofa for an hour after I spoke to Brandon, I decide to go to bed.

I'm just drifting off when I hear the front door to my unit open. At first I'm startled, but then I tell myself that it's probably just Tessa finally coming home. I wait a few minutes, deciding what lecture I should give her, before getting out of bed and putting my housecoat on. I open my bedroom door and scream.

Brandon is standing in front of me.

"Brandon. You scared the hell out of me." I put a hand to my chest.

He smiles that irresistible grin. "I'm sorry, beautiful. I didn't mean to freak you out. I just couldn't sleep until I kissed you good night."

I smile and exhale. "I'm glad you're here."

Brandon grabs me around my waist and pulls me into him, then presses his soft lips against mine. The same shivers rush over me as they did the night we made love.

"Can you stay?" I ask.

He shakes his head. "No, but soon. I have to be up in just a few hours because there's a very important client I'm finishing a job for."

He kisses my forehead and tells me he'll call after he gets off his shift. We say goodnight, and I watch as he walks down the hall to the exit.

Just as I close the door, I look down at the knob, and it hits me—how did Brandon get in the building without me letting him in? How had he gotten in my unit without a key? I am sure I locked the door before bed. I always do.

I make sure the lock is secure, then go back to the bedroom. As I lie in bed, I start to question if I locked the door at all. Maybe I was so preoccupied thinking about Brandon that I just thought I locked it.

I don't mind Brandon dropping by unannounced, especially to surprise me with a kiss good night, but it's never a good idea to have your door unlocked while you sleep. You never know what kind of creeps can get into the building just by waiting for someone to open the main entrance door.

* * *

Standing before the class of less-than-enthused students, I read my interpretation of "The Rime of the Ancient Mariner," a poem written in the 1700s. Afterward, the professor nods in approval and I walk back to my seat.

It's important I do well enough to pass. If I don't, I've not only wasted my time, but more importantly I've lost all the money my parents took from their savings to pay my tuition.

When the class ends, I funnel out of the room behind the other students. Just as I enter the hallway, I feel my phone vibrate in my pocket. As I walk to my next class, I pull out my cell and see a strange number on the display. Veering off into a doorway, I answer the call.

"Hello." I speak loudly to drown out the noise from the other students walking by.

"Is this Sophie?" a woman's voice says.

"Yes. Who's calling?"

The woman tells me that she's with the police, and wants to talk to me about Tessa.

"Did something happen to Tessa? Is she okay?"

The officer asks me when I saw Tessa last, if she said anything out of character, or if there may be any information that would lead her to run away. I tell her everything I know, minus the pregnancy part. The officer then gives me her name, number, and the extension I can reach her at if I hear from Tessa.

When the call ends, I stand feeling completely stunned in the now-empty hallway. I know I should be hustling to my next class, but I can't. The seriousness of Tessa's disappearance just set in.

I can't believe the cops are involved. Tessa's parents must have called them and reported their daughter missing. The funny thing is, Tessa has disappeared many times before and never were the police called. I guess they really believed she was wanting to change her life. I believed her, too.

Instead of going to my class, I walk past the room and head back to my unit. My brain is too frazzled to absorb any in-person lessons right now and I need to be alone to sort out my thoughts.

Back at my place, I call my parents in Scotland, something I usually only do on our scheduled call times of once every couple of weeks.

My mother answers the phone in a groggy voice. I quickly add up the time difference between us and realize it's the middle of the night where they live.

"Mom, sorry I woke you."

"Sophie, are you okay?"

"I'm fine. And I never would've called you, except I wanted to tell you that Tessa is missing."

"What do you mean missing?" My mother's voice gets louder.

"She took off from my unit in the middle of the night and she hasn't been heard from since."

"Oh my God. That's terrible. Have the police been called?"

I tell her that I spoke with Tessa's mother, and how the cops called me just an hour ago to ask questions about Tess.

"Do you know anything that may help them locate her?"

"Absolutely not. I want her found too, Mom."

"I've always liked that girl, but to be honest, I wasn't surprised when she got into trouble when you girls were younger. If I'm honest, I was always quite apprehensive of you chumming around with her."

"I'm older than she is. I was never in any danger of being influenced by Tessa," I lie.

My mother is quiet for a few moments. "Maybe she's into drugs and took off to get blazed up."

"Blazed up? Mom, I don't even know what that means. Blaze up means to light a joint."

"Whatever, Sophie. You know what I meant. All I'm trying to say is that Tessa could be hooked on drugs."

"She's not hooked on anything, except maybe potato chips and pop. The night she disappeared, she was heading to 7/11 to buy snacks. She left a note saying that she'd be right back. When I woke up hours later, she hadn't come back. I agree, in the past she's had a reputation for taking off, but not now. Not in her condition."

As soon as the last words slip out of my mouth, I know I've made a huge mistake.

"Her condition?" my mother repeats.

I sigh. "Just forget about it, Mom, please!"

"Are you saying that Tessa is pregnant?"

I know my mother and how, when she homes in on something, she won't drop it until she gets the information out of you.

"Mom, you can't tell anyone, especially Tessa's parents. Plus, Tessa could have been wrong about being pregnant, I don't really know."

"You need to tell her mother," my mother says sternly. "It's information that could help to locate her daughter."

I shake my head. "How could the fact that Tessa may be pregnant help to locate her? Seriously, Mother!"

"Withholding information is the same as telling a lie."

I tell my mom how I promised Tessa that I wouldn't say anything, then beg her not to tell Mr. and Mrs. Waters anything about their daughter being knocked-up. After a long debate, my mom finally agrees to say nothing, for now.

"I'm sorry I woke you in the middle of the night. I just know that you and Dad are close to the Waterses, and I thought maybe you could call them and console them. And maybe you could re-iterate that I don't know where Tessa is, so it's pointless for them to have the police call me anymore."

My mother agrees, and I thank her, then tell her I love her before hanging up.

I text Brandon, hoping he'll text me back soon. I could really use the distraction right now. I wait for the better part of an hour, with no response.

I spend the next several hours trying to focus enough to do the assignments I missed today. When my concentration wavers and I can't study anymore, I decide to take a drive to the 7/11, even though I realize it's probably pointless. I'm sure the police have already been there and have asked about Tessa. But I just feel the need to go there.

On my way, I text Brandon again and tell him that I'm going to the 7/11 near campus to ask about Tessa.

* * *

The parking lot is full, so I pull into a slip across the lot. Inside, I stand behind a half-dozen students with their arms full of chips and candy. Finally, when it's my turn at cash, I ask the young worker if she was aware of a girl named Tessa Waters, who's been reported missing.

The girl shakes her head and tells me to wait while she goes into the office to ask her boss if he knows anything. A few minutes pass, with more patrons coming into the store and lining up behind me.

Mr. Cooper, the long-time manager of the 7/11 recognizes me as he walks out from the office behind the cash counter. He smiles at me. "Hello."

"Hi. I'm sorry to bother you. I was just wondering if you've heard anything about my friend Tessa. She came in here a lot before, and now she's gone missing."

Mr. Cooper nods his head. "Yes. The police were by and they showed me a picture of the girl. I recognized her right away. But we checked the cameras the evening she went missing, and she did not come into the store."

"That's strange. She walked from the campus to here to buy snacks."

His expression is concerned. "I'm sorry. I wish I could be more help."

"That's okay. But if you do see her, please call the police right away."

As soon as I'm back in my car, my cell phone rings. Hoping it's Brandon, I slide the phone from my pocket and look at the screen.

When I read the name, my body freezes.

Tessa.

With my fingers shaking, I manage to push the answer button on the second ring.

"Hello. Tessa?"

No one answers.

Again, I speak into the phone, this time louder. "Tess? Are you there?"

But she's hung up. Immediately I redial her number, but it goes right to voicemail, where a voice tells me that her messages are full. I take a deep breath and dial her mother's number. Maybe she's heard from Tessa.

It takes three rings for Mrs. Waters to answer. She sounds weak and tired.

"Hello. It's Sophie calling. I'm sorry to bother you, but I just received a call from Tessa and—"

"What? You did? How is she? Where is she?" Her voice is suddenly awake and animated.

"I don't know, because when I answered, she'd already hung up. I tried calling her back, but there was no answer."

Tessa's mother lets out a sob. "But she called you. She's alive. Oh, thank God!"

I can't help but tear up, too. "Yes. Thank God!"

"Please call me once she phones you back, and please tell her to get a hold of her father and me as soon as possible."

"I will. I promise."

"Oh, thank God! I really thought something terrible had happened to her this time." She giggles anxiously. "I guess my mother's intuition isn't working."

"It's going to be okay. I'm sure her phone just died. She'll probably call back once it's charged."

"Yes." She sighs a breath of relief. "I guess I should call the police and let them know we've had contact with her."

I tell her that I'll be in touch, then start the car and drive home.

By the time I park, I'm pissed off at Tessa all over again.

How could she be so selfish in worrying her poor parents half to death? On the phone, it sounded like her mother hadn't slept for days, that poor woman. I could never do that to my mom and dad. It would take years off their life if I put them through the stress that Tessa has put her family through.

Back in my unit, I flop down on the sofa and put my phone on the end table in case she calls me back. Then I take out my laptop and quickly send Mom an email, giving her an update on Tessa.

Brandon calls just as I'm getting up to put a pizza pocket in the microwave.

"Hey, beautiful. How are you?"

It's good to hear his voice. Immediately, my mood lifts. "I'm good. Tessa finally called me, so everyone can finally relax."

"Yeah, I knew she was probably just partying or something."

"You were right. Though, after hearing how upset her mother has been, I almost feel angry with her."

"I agree. She's a selfish girl to do something like that. She needs to grow up and be accountable for her life."

"I know. To be honest, I don't know if I really want to hear all of her excuses for disappearing when she does call back. Now that I know she's probably okay, I'm not so open to the idea of letting her back into my life until she gets herself together."

"I've got a great idea to take your mind off her."

"What?"

"Why don't I come over? I can even stay the night, if you don't get bored of me."

I laugh. "As if that could ever happen. But don't you have to work today?"

"Nah. I've been going pretty hard without a proper day off. I think I deserve some time to myself. Plus, I was up super early touching up a V.I.P. customer's car, so it's not like I haven't done anything today."

"Okay. Great. When are you thinking of coming?"

"I'll tell you what. I'll just have a quick shower, then be on my way. Don't worry about food—we'll order in, okay?"

"Perfect." I put the pizza pockets back into the freezer.

I quickly do my hair and change into a pair of tights and a flattering shirt, then put on just enough make-up to look like I wasn't trying too hard. After I give the place a quick once-over, I sit down and wait.

An hour later, Brandon texts me to come downstairs and let him in the main door. As soon as I see him on the other side of the glass, I feel flushed and excited, and hope I don't look too frumpy.

As soon as I push the door open, he grabs my waist, gives me a kiss, then swoops me up in his arms. Refusing to put me down, he carries me up the stairs to my unit. By the time we're inside, he's trying to hide the fact that he's out of breath.

As soon as he sits on the sofa, I jump on top of him and press my lips against his.

He kisses me back, and soon we're in heavy-petting mode. Brandon uses his restraint and laughs. "If we don't order pizza now, we'll end up making love all night, and I'm starving."

I push back from him. "So, what you're saying is, if you have the chance to make love to me or eat pizza, the food wins?"

"No." He smiles. "You're dessert."

"A little cheesy, but I'll accept it."

He tickles me for a moment, then grabs his phone and calls the pizza joint. As we wait for the delivery, we try everything we can to keep our hands off each other—watch TV, talk about his job and about my classes—until we lose the battle and Brandon carries me into the bedroom. A half-hour later, we're lost in the throes of passion, completely engulfed in the heat of the moment.

It's only after Brandon orgasms and catches his breath that he sits straight up and says, "Oh no. The pizza guy."

He jumps up and grabs his jeans, stuffing one leg inside as he hops half-naked into the front room to grab his phone. I hear him call the pizza place and profusely apologize, then plead for the delivery driver to come back. With no shirt or shoes on, he pokes his head into the doorway and tells me he's going downstairs to meet the driver at the door.

I shake my head and smile, wondering how many students will see him running downstairs half-dressed. I'm sure I'll be the talk of the building tomorrow.

I get up and grab plates and napkins, then place them on the coffee table. After ten minutes, Brandon returns with a victorious smile. "I got it." He holds up a pizza box. "But I had to give the delivery guy a pretty big tip."

We share the pizza and tidy up before heading back to the bedroom for another hot session of lovemaking.

* * *

I can't believe how into him I am, I think as I watch him sleep.

It's still dark out, and I at least want to make him coffee before he has to get up and go to work. As quietly as I can, I inch out of the bed and creep out to the living room.

After putting the coffee on, I walk over to the window and look out. As the morning sun slowly floods the ground, the colours of the leaves come to life, bright yellows and reds almost glowing as the sun dances from branch to branch.

When the coffee is finished percolating, I grab two cups from the cupboard and, after adding the right measurements of sugar and cream, I tiptoe back into the bedroom carrying the warm drinks.

Standing beside the bed, I intentionally clear my throat, trying to wake Brandon, but he doesn't move. Then I softly whisper his name, but still no response. Finally, I speak at a normal volume. "Brandon, it's the coffee fairy. Time to wake up."

And with that, I finally see movement as he brings an arm up and covers his eyes to keep the light out.

"Wakey wakey," I say happily. "It's time to get out of bed."

Brandon grumbles, then in a groggy voice says, "Come back to bed with me. Let's just curl up together and shut the world out."

I laugh. "That's a great idea, but you don't want to lose your job and I have classes to go to."

He sighs loudly. "It sucks being a grown-up."

We laugh. He finally sits up and looks at the cups in my hand. "Wow, you actually brought me a coffee in bed? That's awesome. You're a cool girl, Sophie."

I hand him his coffee, then carefully sit next to him with mine.

"I have to go away for a bit," he announces suddenly. "I'll be leaving tomorrow morning."

Instantly, my happy feelings are gone. "You're going away? For how long?"

"A week. I have to head to Victoria to meet with a guy about a business opportunity."

"Oh." I try to hide my disappointment.

"Why don't you come with me? I'll only be busy for a small portion of each day. The rest of the time we can spend together, walking on the beach or snuggled up in bed."

"Me? Go to Vancouver Island for a week? I wish. But I have to go to classes and do assignments. If I were away for a whole week, I'd fall majorly behind."

Brandon frowns, then reaches out and touches my leg. "Okay. If that's what you want to do, I guess I'll see you in about a week."

I can't imagine him going away. I can't imagine not being able to make love to him, or talk to him face to face. But there's no way I'd be able to leave school for seven whole days, then try to play catch up. I'm not that great of a student.

I watch him as he quickly finishes his coffee, then jumps up and gets dressed. I feel sad that he's leaving, and I can tell that he's disappointed with my answer.

"I'd love nothing more than to go with you," I say.

"If that's the truth, then you would figure out a way."

"That's not true, Brandon. I just know how badly that would set me back. They give a ton of homework in these classes, and there's instruction for every paper I have to do."

"Okay then." He gives me a fake smile. "Just forget I brought it up."

I sit quietly as he puts his shoes on. When he's finished, he walks over to me. "Stand up and give me a hug. I've got to get going."

I place my mug on the bedside table. Then, with my head down, I wrap my arms around his waist. "I'm sorry. I really do want to go with you."

"Please stop saying that," he says, then walks out of the room. I follow him to the front door. Just as he turns the knob, he looks back at me and smiles. "It's too bad, we would've had a blast."

"Let me think on it. Maybe there's a way. I just need some time to—"

Brandon grabs me in his arms and lifts me off the ground. "That's my girl. I love the fact that you're willing to try. That tells me a lot about the way you feel about me. About us."

He kisses me, then says he'll call at the end of the day.

Once he leaves and the door is closed, the reality of what I've just sort of agreed to hits me. I'm already behind in my classes because of how frazzled I got when the cops called me and I took the day off.

A whole week away from classes is going to sink me. I hate to lie, but if I do go with Brandon, I'll have no choice but to come up with a big load of BS so I don't get thrown out of my courses.

* * *

I dedicate the next several hours to homework, only stopping for a quick bite and a drink of water. When I glance at the time, I'm surprised to see it's almost 5PM. With my eyes strained from reading, and my back sore from bending over the computer all day, I finally finish all of the outstanding essays.

Stretching out on my bed, I thumb through my phone to check any text messages I may have missed. There's nothing. For the next few minutes, I try to concoct the best lie I can to get out of classes, but I can't think of anything believable. I'm a terrible liar.

Flickering noises come from the window. I look out and notice the soft rain streaming down the pane. My eyes follow the water as it trails down the glass, and my thoughts wander to Brandon.

I imagine what our mini-vacation would be like. I picture us laughing and teasing each other as we walk along the beach. I see us having romantic dinners, sitting side by side in a cool seaside restaurant. And the sex, at night, intertwined on white sheets as our bodies gyrate in rhythm with one another. I smile just thinking about it.

I know now that as much as I'll feel bad for telling a lie to cut classes, I can't miss the opportunity to spend time with Brandon.

I start planning which outfits to bring along and which ones are the most flattering. I want him to see me at my best, and not the normal frumpy girl that I'm used to being. I just wish I had time to go shopping before the morning. I could've bought some sexy pieces at the lingerie store and really surprise him. Unfortunately, Abbotsford rolls up the sidewalks pretty early most days, so I guess I'll just have to make do with what I have.

* * *

It's 10PM when I finally get a text from Brandon. He tells me he's too tired to chat on the phone, but he'll swing by to pick me up in the morning.

I still have to pack and email each one of my professors with the only lie I could think of to excuse me from classes for a week—my grandmother died, and I have to go to the Island for the service with my family.

It's a ridiculous lie, and if my professors ask me about her the next time I see them, they'll know I was snowballing them for sure. My mother always said that I couldn't lie to save my life; I have too many tells on my face. She never told me what they were, I guess because then I could try and change them.

I slip into a warm bubble bath, light a scented candle, and listen to a compilation CD of soft rock. I can't wait to spend time with Brandon on the Island. I'm so excited about the trip, but I've been a hermit for so long, I have no one to share the news with.

One person I could share things with is Tessa, but she's still M.I.A., no doubt with some guy she met, partying her face off. The only other person I spill my guts to is my mom, and there's no way I could tell her about taking off school for a week to be with a guy I just met. She'd have a bird.

Not to mention, it's her and Dad's hard-earned cash that's financing my degree. If they knew I was putting my education in jeopardy, they'd be devastated. So far, in my twenty-three years, I've managed not to be a huge disappointment to them, and I don't want to change that now.

Chapter Six

My phone chirps at 7AM. It's Brandon, telling me to meet him downstairs in half an hour.

I quickly hop out of bed and get changed, then fix my hair and makeup. I barely have time for a quick cup of coffee before it's time to grab my suitcase and head down to the entrance, where Brandon waits.

* * *

As soon as I exit the truck, a strong breeze whips over the wave-soaked car deck, making it a struggle to push against the wind. When I make it to the back of the truck, Brandon walks around the tailgate and grabs a hold of my arm.

By the time we walk up the long stairs to the upper deck of the ferry, my hair looks like it's been backcombed and I resemble Marge Simpson. Brandon laughs when he looks at me, then points to the sign that says *ladies washroom*.

Once inside, I take a brush from my purse and do my best to tame my wild hair. As I stand in front of the mirror, I notice other women walk in with the same wind-blown look, so I don't feel too bad.

When I walk out of the bathroom, Brandon is standing against the wall with his arms folded. I can see women checking him out as they walk by. He smiles when he sees me, then pulls me in for a tight hug. *Eat your heart out, girls. He's all mine.*

Brandon leads me to the cafeteria, and after getting a couple of muffins and coffee, we find a table to sit at. He starts to tell me about how much fun we're going to have when a tall guy with brown shoulder-length hair approaches the table, a red-headed scruffy lady in tow. They both look to be in their thirties.

"Hey, Brandon," the guy says. "What's up, man?"

Brandon looks up at him. "Hey, Ryder. Have a seat."

Ryder glances at me, and as soon as our eyes meet, a chill runs down my back. There's something strange about this guy. He looks like he hasn't had a shower in a long time, and his eyes tell me he's a shyster who's up to no good.

The woman sits next to me at the table, and doesn't make eye contact until Ryder introduces us. "Sophie, this is my old lady, Sylvie."

She glances at me with disinterest, then looks away.

Brandon grabs my hand. "These are the roommates I told you about."

I nod. "Oh. I see. And they are coming along with us?" I pray he says no.

"Yeah. Ryder is in on this business deal with me. They'll be staying at the same motel as us." He grins. "Don't worry, they'll be in a separate room."

I smile, trying to hide my disappointment. "Oh. I didn't realize we were going over with another couple."

"Didn't I mention that?"

"No, I guess you forgot to."

"Why? Is that a problem?" Ryder sneers.

"No. Of course not. I'm just surprised, is all."

As Ryder and Brandon talk, any excitement I had about the vacation quickly diminishes. Even though the boat ride is only an hour and a half long, it feels like a hell of a lot longer while I force fake grins and pretend that I'm not annoyed. I try to engage Sylvie in conversation, but she pretends she doesn't hear and resumes ignoring me.

Finally, an automated voice comes through the overhead speakers, telling all of the passengers to return to their vehicles as we near the Departure Bay Terminal.

Back in the truck, Brandon pulls me close and kisses me, but I must be emitting negative vibes because right away he pulls back and studies me. "Everything okay, babe?"

I shrug. "I guess so. I just thought it would be the two of us for the week. Now, there's your pal Ryder and his girlfriend, too."

Brandon grins. "They won't be anywhere near us, I promise. During the day, Ryder will need to accompany me to a couple of quick meetings. After that, he'll go back to his room, and we'll be in ours. Okay?"

I sigh. "Okay."

"Now slide over here." He points to the gap between us.

Brandon and I are locked in a long kiss when there's a hard rap on his window, making me jump back and gasp. It's Ryder.

Brandon looks annoyed as he unrolls the window. "What the hell, man. Can't you see we're busy?"

"Sorry, man, I just wanted to know if I'm following you once we're off the ferry, or if you're following me."

Brandon shakes his head in disbelief. "Ryder, where are you parked?"

He points down the row of cars behind us. "Back there."

"Right. Then isn't it logical that you'll be following us?"

He shrugs and thinks for a second. Then he laughs goofily. "Oh, yeah. Okay. No problem." He walks away.

Brandon looks over at me, then puts his hands up and laughs. "No words."

The ferry traffic drains off of the vessel and we slowly follow the long trail of vehicles up to the main highway. Brandon checks his rear-view mirror to make sure his friends are following us, then takes the turn South toward Victoria. I ask him for the name of the town we're going to, and he tells me it's a small, artsy place called Duncan.

As we make our way down the road, the sky opens up into the most remarkable blue. As he drives, Brandon tucks his hand between my thighs. If a guy had rested his hand there in the past I would inch away, but everything Brandon does feels natural.

A couple of hours pass before we enter the town of Duncan. We drive past small buildings painted with brightly coloured murals, then take a small side road that runs parallel to the ocean until we reach a light blue, older-looking motel.

Brandon tells me to sit tight while he goes to the office to check us in. While he's gone, Ryder and Sylvie pull up in a small white car and park beside us.

Ryder gets out of the driver's side. As he passes on his way to the motel office, he stops to leer at me through the window, making my skin crawl.

* * *

For the next three days, everything goes much as Brandon said it would. After he gets home from his meetings, we pick up or order in dinner, then take walks on the beach, hand in hand. Last night, after we made love, he fell asleep and I found myself watching him, an overwhelming wave of emotion crashing over me. At that moment, I knew I was falling deeply in love.

* * *

Before he leaves, Brandon leans over and kisses me. "What are you going to do today?"

I smile. "I thought I'd walk around town for a while. I'll scope out a restaurant we can eat at when you get back from your meetings."

"That's a great idea. I'll be starving by then. Just be ready to go around five, and I'll swing by here to pick you up."

After Brandon leaves, I have a quick shower, then put my hair in a ponytail and walk to the center of town. It's not yet ten in the morning, so there are lots of people bustling about in the small streets. It seems everyone I walk past either says hello or smiles and nods, something you don't see a lot on the mainland.

I walk until I come to a small red building, marked *Museum*. I go inside and am immediately blown away by the colourful and interesting displays of Indigenous artwork on the walls.

It isn't long before one of the employees approaches, a soft-spoken woman in her sixties. She gives me the history of the pieces, then shows me a large agriculture exhibit just off the main room. When I've seen everything and have heard a story to go with each artifact, I thank the woman for the tour and leave.

Standing at the exit, I check my watch and see that two hours have passed—I've still got quite a bit of time before Brandon gets back to the motel.

After stopping at a boutique bakery and getting a croissant and a bottle of water, I make my way over to the marina and find a bench overlooking the crystal-clear water. There are several colourful houseboats in the centre of the marina, and surrounding them are sailboats in every size with a few powerboats mixed in.

As I eat my snack, a piece of pastry falls to the ground and catches the eye of a nearby gull. Slowly, the bird waddles toward my feet, looking at the morsel of food, then up at me. I take care not to make any sudden movements. Carefully, the gull sizes me up as it nears the food.

I startle and squeal when the bird lunges at my feet, grabbing the piece of bun and fluttering its wings as it walks away.

Just then, an elderly woman with a small dog heads up the path toward me. She slows as she approaches. "Do you mind if I sit here?" She points to the bench.

I quickly scoot over. "Of course not. There's lots of room."

She tells me her name is Marg, and I introduce myself. Then, she sees a gull fly overhead and immediately scoops up her tiny dog and places it on her lap. "If we're sitting, I always pick her up. There are a lot of bald eagles and hawks that will try and snatch up my little Snowball if I'm not careful." She strokes the little cotton ball of a dog.

I nod, not really sure if her fear is logical or paranoia.

The woman asks me where I'm from. When I tell her I live in Abbotsford, she gives me a full history of her late husband's family, who was also from the Fraser Valley.

As much as her story seems to drag on with no real point in sight, I'm happy to be talking to Marg. She's nice, and I'm thoroughly content sitting in such a beautiful environment.

When she finally finishes talking about herself, she asks me how long my parents have lived in Abbotsford, and what I do for a living. When she finds out I'm a student, she asks right away why I'm not at school. I tell her that I'm here with my boyfriend because he has business in the area.

Leaving no stone unturned, Marg inquires about Brandon, wanting to know the details of his work. And that's when I realize I know very little about what he's doing in Duncan. I just understood it had something to do with cars.

After a few more minutes, Marg tells me it was nice to meet me, but she must be going. She gets up, places her dog on the ground, and they continue up the path.

* * *

Vibrant strokes of orange and red trail behind the evening sun as it fades into the horizon. I've spent the last hour and a half doing my hair and makeup so I look good for Brandon when he takes me out for dinner tonight.

He was supposed to be here an hour ago, but he hasn't replied to any of my messages. I assume something work-wise tied him up. Either way, my stomach is rumbling as I'm forced to sit and wait for him.

Hours tick by, and there's still no sign of him. I've tried texting and calling, but to no avail. Time passes slowly, and when the clock hits midnight, I'm both pissed off and worried. What the hell could be taking him so long?

I wait an extra half hour, then decide to walk to the gas station up the road for some snacks to quiet my empty stomach.

Thankfully the moon is bright tonight, and I huddle in my sherpa as I walk along the narrow road to the gas station. All the while, I'm hoping that I'll see the headlights appear from Brandon's truck—no such luck.

After buying a bag of chips and a sandwich, I head back to the motel. When I reach the parking lot, I don't see Brandon's or Ryder's vehicles anywhere. Discouraged, I walk up the stairs to our room on the second floor. Before I enter, I notice that the light is on in Sylvie and Ryder's room. *Maybe she's heard from the guys?*

I walk to their door and rap once, then take a deep breath. I hate to disturb anyone this time of night, especially when I got such a cold vibe from her on the ferry.

I wait and wait, but she doesn't answer. Again, I knock, this time a little harder.

Finally, I hear someone rustling inside. She opens the door a crack, only part of her face visible. When she recognizes me, she pulls the door fully open. Her hair is frizzy and her skin is pale, making her appear even more intense.

"What do you want?" she barks.

I take a step back. "I'm sorry to bother you, Sylvie. It's just that I haven't heard from Brandon, and I thought maybe you had an idea of—"

"Do I look like a damn babysitter to you?"

"No. Of course not. I'm sorry I bothered you."

I quickly turn and walk toward my room with a lump in my throat. I'm not used to people being so mean to me.

"Hey, come back here," she orders.

I take another deep breath, then turn to face her. "Yes?" I say, choking back tears.

"Aren't you a student?"

I nod.

"Then you've got no business being here."

Caught off guard, I can't think of a response. All I can do is stare at her. It's only when I see approaching headlights reflecting off her face that I break our locked gaze, turning to look at the road. When I glance back at Sylvie, she scowls and slams the door.

I walk back to my room just as Brandon pulls up. Normally I'd run to the mirror to fix my makeup and hair before he sees me, but right now I'm feeling so pissed off at him and so insulted at how Sylvie spoke to me, I couldn't care less how I look.

I stand by the window just as he walks in. His eyes are bloodshot and he looks like he's been drinking. "Hey, beautiful. Come and give me a kiss."

Ryder passes behind him. "No thanks," Ryder yells.

Brandon laughs. "Not you, asshole," he says, before shutting the door and grinning at me.

"I don't really feel like kissing you right now."

His expression changes to one of confusion. "Why not?"

"Let's start with where you were all night. You told me you'd be home at dinner time, and we'd go out together. Then, to make matters worse, you didn't answer my texts or calls, so I didn't know what was going on."

Brandon sighs, then sits on the bed. "I'm so sorry, babe. I forgot my phone in the glove compartment of my truck, and our meeting went late. Afterward, our new partner took us out for drinks in his car. I had no access to my cell. I'm so sorry."

I shake my head and fold my arms in front of me. "I guess I understand, sort of. But to really top my crappy night off, I went to Sylvie's room to ask if she'd heard from you and Ryder, and she was really mean to me."

Brandon stands up and looks cross. "What do you mean? What did she say to you?"

I feel a little better when I see how upset he is over how Sylvie treated me. I tell him what she said and, more importantly, how she said it.

"That's completely unacceptable," he says. "She's just jealous because you're so pretty and she looks like a hag."

"I don't know. I think her hatred for me runs deeper than that."

"Trust me. She's a bitter old broad who hates everyone, especially younger women. It's not personal. She's a grade-A bitch."

Brandon walks over to me and wraps his arms around my waist. "I'm mad about you Sophie. Please don't be upset with me." He fakes a goofy frown.

I start to laugh. "Just please don't disappear on me for that long again."

"Deal." He kisses me.

I decide to have a quick shower while Brandon lies on the bed. In the bathroom, I've just taken my clothes off when I hear the door to the hotel room open and close.

I peek out the bathroom door and see that Brandon is no longer on the bed. I immediately tense up, but then I see his phone and wallet on the nightstand, so I relax and close the door. He likely went to the pop machine or forgot something in his truck.

By the time I'm out of the bathroom, he's back on the bed. He smiles when he sees me, then motions for me to lie next to him.

We kiss for a while and end up naked beneath the covers. At first, Brandon is hot and heavy to make love to me. However, it's obvious that he's fading fast, likely from the booze he consumed at his meeting.

* * *

Dark clouds roll over the sky and a downpour of rain soon follows.

Brandon takes me for brunch, even though he looks hungover and food is probably the last thing on his mind. As soon as we get to a small diner in town, he goes up to the counter and buys a container of Aspirin.

We sit at a table beside a large window overlooking the beach. The waitress walks up with two menus in one hand and a pot of coffee in the other. Once we order bacon and eggs and our mugs are filled with coffee, Brandon reaches over the table and grabs my hands in his.

"I am so sorry for last night, Soph. I hope you've forgiven me. I promise you, it won't happen like that again. If I have a late meeting, I'll make sure I have my cell with me."

"It's okay. I just hope your hangover isn't too bad."

"I deserve it, after making you wait all night for me."

"No, you don't. It was an easy mistake, what happened. Let's just move past it."

"You know what? You're like, the perfect girl. I've never met anyone like you."

I smile, feeling a little embarrassed.

He smiles coyly. "I've been giving something a lot of thought, and it's taken me days to work up the courage to talk to you about it."

"Brandon, don't be silly. You can talk to me about anything."

He takes a deep breath. "Okay. Here it goes. When we get back to the city, I want you to move in with me."

I immediately sit back, and my mouth drops open.

He's looking deep into my eyes. I know I have to say something, but I'm so shocked, I have no words.

Thankfully the waitress walks over with our breakfast, giving me a moment to catch my bearings. Brandon barely looks at his plate, keeping his focus on me. "Well? Aren't you going to say anything?"

"Yeah. It's just that you took me by surprise."

He shakes his head. "You hate the idea."

I lean over the table and touch his hand. "No. I don't hate the idea at all. It's just that I didn't expect you to ask me to move in so soon."

A serious look comes over his face. "I know we haven't known each other long, but when you know, you know."

"Know what?"

"I'm falling in love with you, Sophie."

My chest flutters, and all of a sudden my body feels weightless. "I feel the same way."

He squeezes my hand. "Good! Then moving in together should be a no-brainer."

"I thought you lived above the shop. Do you think there's enough room for me there?"

"No, silly. I'd never ask you to move into that crappy place. Ryder and Sylvie found us a farmhouse just outside of Abbotsford, it's great."

All of the warmth I've been feeling quickly fades. "Ryder and Sylvie would be living there also?"

"Well of course, sweetie. I told you that we were looking for a place a while ago."

"I remember. It's just that—"

"You don't want to live with them."

"No. I really don't. Sylvie seems like she could ride a broom, and Ryder gives me the creeps."

Brandon chuckles. "Yeah, they lack in social graces, I can't argue that point.

Thankfully, the farmhouse is big enough that we can live in one area, and they can live in the other. We will barely see them."

"Really? I guess that doesn't sound too bad."

"It's going to be great." He smiles. "And most importantly, we'll be together."

"Yeah. You're right."

"As I make more money, it won't be long before we can get our own place, especially now that we've sealed the deal with this business partner here."

Then, I remember Marg, the elderly lady I met by the marina yesterday. I think about how she asked me about Brandon's line of work, and how I couldn't tell her much about it.

"What will you be doing with your new job?" I ask. "It has something to do with cars, right?"

"That's right. I'll be starting my own business fixing up cars, which is another reason the farmhouse is perfect. I'll have the main garage to work in, plus two big barns for extra space."

Just then, the door to the diner opens, and right away I recognize Ryder as he saunters in. Sylvie is right behind him. Her red hair is tucked under a baseball cap and she's wearing oversized dark sunglasses, which strikes me as odd, considering how cloudy and miserable it is outside.

Ryder looks at us, and Brandon nods. I let out a huge sigh when they pass by and sit at another table.

Brandon notices my glum expression as I look at the couple. "Hey," he says, prompting me to shift my eyes back to him. "Don't worry about them. It's you and me, okay? That's all that matters."

Back at the motel, Brandon lies with me, and we watch TV for a couple of hours before he has to go to another meeting. I pretend to pout, sticking out my bottom lip. "I don't want you to go and leave me all alone. It's boring here by myself."

He puts on his leather jacket, then leans over me on the bed. "I know it hasn't been much fun while I'm working. Trust me, I'd rather be here with you. The good news is, today is the last day I'll have to go to meetings. After this, we can stay here another day or two, or we can head back to the mainland. It's up to you."

I smile and kiss him. He gets up, throws twenty dollars on the bedside table, and leaves.

I flip through the channels for the next hour before deciding to go visit the pop machine on the main floor.

As soon as I open the door and walk outside, a cold wind carrying beads of hard rain pushes against me, prompting me to grab the railing on my way down the stairs. I quickly make my way to the soda machine and dig in my pockets for change. After inserting two loonies, I select a can of Coke and am just bending over to grab it from the tray when I hear someone approach from behind. I quickly straighten up and turn around.

It's Sylvie. She has her arms crossed over a thin tank top. As cold as it is out, it doesn't seem to be bothering her.

A gust of wind suddenly blows around us, causing her frizzy red hair to lift and fully expose her face. That's when I notice a large purple and red bruise around her right eye.

"Oh, wow, Sylvie. Your eye. What happened?"

"Mind your own business."

I maneuver around her, then make my way back to my room.

Once inside, I sit on the bed and think about seeing Sylvie at the diner earlier. She had on those big dark sunglasses. I guess I now know why she was wearing them.

I hope her creep of a boyfriend didn't hit her.

I'm just about to grab the remote control when there's a knock at the door. I slowly get up and pull back the curtain on the window to look outside, but no one's there. I then put on the security chain and open the door slowly.

Looking through the gap, I still don't see anyone. Then I look down, and see a can of Coke on the ground in front of me.

I realize then that I was so taken aback by Sylvie's black eye and how she snapped at me, I'd forgotten my pop in the machine. I unlatch my door and open it, peering outside. Sylvie is just entering her room. She glances at me without expression, then walks inside and closes the door.

After a few hours, the rain outside dissipates and I decide to go for a walk to stretch my legs. Just as I get my shoes and coat on, I hear Brandon talking outside. When I open the door, I see Ryder first and Brandon behind him. He's carrying a small rose in his hand.

Brandon says goodbye to his creepy friend, then smiles when he sees me. "Hey, beautiful. Look what I got you." He passes me the flower.

He maneuvers me backward into the room. Before I know it, our coats are off and we're kissing on the bed.

With our lips pressed together, we struggle to kick our shoes off. I laugh as I hear each shoe hit the floor. After a few moments, he stops kissing me and looks into my eyes. "I love you, Sophie."

His words combined with the softness of his tone rush through me. "I love you, too."

Chapter Seven

I awaken to the annoying sound of thrash metal as Brandon's phone lights up on the nightstand. I roll over and lightly push against him. "Your phone is ringing."

He moans and, without looking, reaches for his cell. I lay my head back on the pillow as he puts his phone to his ear. "What's up, Ryder?"

As Brandon talks on his cell, I lean over and check my phone for the time. It's 7AM.

After a few more words, Brandon ends the call and rolls over to cuddle me. "I'm sorry he woke us so early. I've got to go soon and load up my truck. It looks like we'll be leaving today after all."

I roll over and face him. "But I thought you said we could stay a couple more days if we wanted?"

"That's what I thought, but our new partner wants to get business rolling as soon as possible."

He pulls me tightly into him for a few more minutes, then gets up to have a shower. I get dressed and finger-comb my hair. Once he's out of the bathroom, I mention how yesterday I saw Sylvie at the pop machine, and she had a big shiner.

"Oh, yeah. That's right. She rolled off the bed in her sleep and hit her face on the nightstand."

"Hit her face on the nightstand? Is that what Ryder told you?"

"Yeah. Why?"

"I don't know. Doesn't that sound a bit hard to believe?"

He shrugs. "Not really. I've managed to get bruises in a lot sillier ways than that."

"You don't think there's any possibility that he hit her?"

"Ryder?" Brandon sounds surprised. "He's a quirky guy, but he'd never hit Sylvie. No matter how difficult she can be."

As Brandon gets dressed, he tells me he'll only be gone a short while before coming to pick me up. "Don't forget to pack all of your things. If you notice anything I've forgotten, please just throw it in with your stuff." He gives me a kiss, then walks out the door.

Dutifully, I pack up my belongings. Once I finish, I decide to send my parents a quick email to say hello. I neglect to mention leaving school for a week, and definitely don't mention Brandon, my new boyfriend, and how we've shacked up in a motel together.

I know, at some point, I'll need to tell them about my new relationship, probably the same time I mention we're moving in together. I might as well rip that band aid off all at once.

Although my father is super cheap, and bitched and moaned about the money he had to fork over for me to live in residential, I know he'd rather pay double than see me move in with a guy. My parents are great, but they're seriously old-school when it comes to relationships, especially where I'm concerned.

It's not quite noon when I hear Brandon's voice coming up the stairs. I open the door before he has time to knock. He's soaking wet, the rain coming down in sheets behind him. "Hey, beautiful. Are you all packed up?"

I nod, then kiss him on his wet cheek as he walks in. "Are we going to stop for breakfast in Duncan before we leave?"

"No time. We'll have to get a bite on the ferry."

Brandon grabs his small gym bag and my suitcase, and we walk downstairs to the truck. As I wait for him to open my door, I look up one floor and notice Ryder and Sylvie leaving their room. She's lugging all the bags while all he carries is his cell phone and her purse.

What a total shit he is.

Tall waves crash over the bow as the ferry rocks and shakes. Feeling a little uneasy in the truck, I slide closer to Brandon. He looks at me and winks. "We're okay, beautiful. Would you feel better if we went upstairs?"

I nod, hoping being up top will calm my nerves.

We get out of the truck and Brandon walks around to my side. Just then, a ferry worker wearing a safety vest walks up and tells Brandon that one of the ties holding the tarp over the back of the truck has come undone, then offers to help refasten it.

To my surprise, Brandon immediately responds in an ornery tone, telling the man to stay away from his truck and that he'll handle it himself.

I watch the worker walk away, feeling bad for him. He was only being kind, and certainly didn't deserve to be spoken to so harshly.

I fold my arms around me and shiver while Brandon secures the tarp. Once he's finished, he takes my hand and leads me to the staircase.

Once upstairs, I notice that despite the swaying motion of the boat, nobody seems too concerned. People sit calmly, reading or talking to one another. I calm down a little, and Brandon finds us a seat near the front.

Still feeling confused about how he treated the ferry worker, I ask him why he was so rude.

"I didn't want the guy snooping under the tarp," he explains. "Some of those car parts are very expensive."

I wonder why he'd worry that a ferry worker would steal car parts. Where would he even put them? But I say nothing. I don't want Brandon to think I'm challenging him.

Brandon gets up and tells me he's going to find the bathroom. Once he's gone, I slide my phone out of my pocket and am just about to play a game when the phone alerts me to an incoming call. It takes me a moment to recognize the number as Tessa's mother.

As soon as I answer, the phone starts cutting out. I look at the screen and see that there's only one bar, so I walk around, trying to get a stronger signal. When I reach the side of the ferry, the signal is stronger, and I can hear Mrs. Waters' voice.

"Are you there?" I say loudly.

"Yes. Where are you, Sophie?" Her voice is weak and tired.

Oh no. If I tell her I'm on the ferry, she'll want to know where I've been. It wouldn't be a problem, if she didn't speak to my parents. "I'm in a bad area right now. The phone might lose the connection again." I debate hanging up before she asks me any more questions.

"Can you call me when your phone is working better? It's important."

"Sure." I try to calculate how much longer the ferry ride will be. "I should be able to get better reception in about an hour."

"That's fine. I'll be here." She hangs up.

When I get back to our seats, Brandon is back and looking around. When he sees me, he smiles and sits down. I sit next to him and explain about the phone call.

My stomach grumbles, and I ask Brandon if we can go to the cafeteria. He shakes his head and tells me that when the seas are rough, everything on the ferry closes as a safety precaution. "If you're really starving, they have a few vending machines I can get snacks from."

I decline, knowing the last thing I need right now on the rocking boat is a belly full of junk food.

* * *

I'm grateful to be disembarking from the rollercoaster sailing we just endured. I sit close to Brandon as we drive off the car deck and follow the traffic up the highway.

I check my phone and see that the connection is finally good, so I dial Mrs. Walters. I'm positive she just wants to know if I've heard from Tessa again, and I don't look forward to telling her I haven't. Brandon turns down the stereo so I can hear properly.

The phone clicks as she picks up. "Hello?"

"It's Sophie. My phone is okay to talk now."

"Hi, Sophie. How are you?"

"I'm okay. You sound a bit tired, though. Are you doing okay?"

"I'm on a lot of medication at the moment."

"Oh no. I hope you're not sick."

There's a long silence. Then she says, "They found Tessa."

"Oh. That's great. Who found her?"

"The police."

"Oh no. Was she in trouble?"

"No. They found her body."

My mouth drops open. Suddenly, my vision narrows and my head starts spinning. "I don't understand."

"I can't go into it anymore right now. I'm too woozy from the pills. I just wanted you to know that Tessa is gone. I spoke to your mother last night, and I told her what the police told me. I have to go now."

"Mrs. Waters? Please don't hang up. What happened to Tessa?"

But she's already ended the call.

"Shit! Shit! Shit!" I holler.

"Sophie, what's wrong?" Brandon exclaims.

"I don't get it." I put my hands over my face and rock back and forth.

Brandon pulls the truck over, then grabs my hands and pulls them down so he can see me. "What the hell happened? Are you okay?"

"Tessa was found dead."

Brandon doesn't say anything for a few moments. He just puts his arms around me and pulls me close.

Tears flow down my cheeks. "I've got to call my mom and find out what happened."

My hands are shaking as I scroll down through the contact list on my phone. Once I dial, I sit back and force a deep breath.

My mother picks up right away. "Sophie. It's about time you called back."

"What are you talking about? I never got any calls from you."

"I tried to reach you, but your phone didn't even ring. It just went straight to voicemail. Didn't you get my messages? I left three of them."

"No, I didn't. I don't know what happened, though my phone has been acting weird lately."

"Never mind. That doesn't matter. I take it you've heard from Tessa's parents?"

"Yes. I've just got off the phone with Mrs. Waters. I just can't believe that Tessa is gone. She told me that she called you with the news. Did she give you any details? Was it suicide?"

"No, it wasn't suicide. They found her out at Cultus Lake. Apparently, she had been gone for a number of days. A couple of joggers spotted her body in some bushes beside a walkway out there."

"This is just unbelievable, Mom. It all seems so surreal."

"Can you imagine how her parents feel?"

"I know. Her mom sounded right out of it. The poor woman." Tears stream down my cheeks.

"Apparently Tessa had been strangled. They found her purse just a few feet away from where she was lying. I guess that must be how they identified her."

"Do the police have any idea who could've done it?"

"No. From what I understand, they don't have any leads yet."

I let out a sob. "This is just the worst. Poor Tessa."

"I'm going to come out there for a week. Your father will be staying here."

"Really, Mom?" The thought of seeing her makes me cry even more. I miss her so much.

"I'll stay with you, if that's okay?"

"Of course. Does Mrs. Waters know you're coming to support her?"

"She does, yes."

We talk for a few more minutes before I tell her I have to go, and I'll call her later.

I barely say a word on the drive back to campus. I just stare out the passenger window in denial. How could Tessa really be gone? And what was she doing at Cultus Lake? Did she know the person—or people—who ended her young life? Questions keep rolling through my mind.

"Do you want me to stay with you tonight?" Brandon finally said, snapping me out of my daze.

I look up and see the entrance to my building. "Oh. We're here already. That was fast."

"Sophie, I don't think you should be alone right now."

"I don't know. I can't think. I'm not sure what I need or don't need right now." Tears are rolling down my cheeks again.

He holds me for a few moments, then pulls back and looks into my eyes, wiping my cheeks. "Do you remember what I told you at the restaurant yesterday?"

I shake my head.

"It's you and me, right?"

I nod.

"That means whatever happens, bad or good, we'll go through it together. I can't leave you like this. All I have to do is unload the back of the truck, and I'll be right back, okay?"

I nod. "Okay. Thanks."

Brandon puts the four-way blinkers on, then helps me upstairs with my bag. After giving me a heartfelt hug and kissing me on the forehead, he promises to be back as soon as possible.

Standing in the unit alone, I realize that the place looks different to me now. I wasn't even gone a week, yet the energy in here has somehow changed. It feels cold and lifeless. Maybe because, in the back of my mind, I know Tessa will never get the chance to go back to her courses, and she'll never again be my roommate.

I walk to the sofa and flop out. I think about the last time I saw her, and how she was sorry for being a pain in the butt. I should've been nicer to her, instead of being so annoyed.

Restless, I get up and walk into the bathroom. I study myself in the mirror. The makeup I meticulously applied this morning is sitting in smudges below my eyes. I look ashen and stressed. I run the water in the tub, then go to my room and grab clean jogging pants and a hoodie. I feel so much colder than usual.

As I lie with my head on the back of the tub, I think about when I went to the 7/11 and spoke to Mr. Cooper about Tessa. How when I left, my phone rang and it was Tessa...or at least, I thought it was her. Thinking back, I can't be sure now that it was even her. There was no one there when I answered.

For a moment, I wonder if I should call the police and tell them about the call, but then I remember that I already told Mrs. Waters about it. I'm sure she'd informed the police already.

My stomach grumbles as I lie on my side, my legs pulled up to my chest as I rock back and forth.

* * *

A hard rap on the door jolts me out of my sleep.

I quickly sit up and look over at the clock. It's 10PM.

I'm getting out of bed when I hear an even louder knock coming from the front door. I hope it isn't one of the girls from down the hall. The last thing I want to do is paste on a fake smile and be all cheery. Though, it'd be worse if they've already heard about Tessa and are coming by to give their condolences. I couldn't handle that right now. It's too soon.

I stand at the door, not opening it yet. "Hello?"

"It's me, Soph. Open up."

Thank God. It's Brandon. I open the door, and he's standing with a small backpack flung over his shoulder and a brown take-out food bag in his hand. "Did I wake you?" he asks.

I shrug and walk back into the bedroom to lie down. I can hear Brandon in the front room opening up the take-out bag and getting dishes out. Soon after, he walks in carrying two plates. He carefully sits on the bed beside me. "Soph, you haven't eaten anything all day. Will you please sit up and eat with me?" His voice is soft and caring.

"I don't think I can. I'm sorry. My stomach feels off right now."

"I understand, but you've got to try to get even a little bit down. It'll make you feel better."

Hunger is the last thing I feel right now, but to appease him, I sit up and take one of the plates. "Thanks." I look down at what looks to be chow mein and fried rice.

"I have something that might help with your nerves." He quickly goes to the fridge, then comes back and hands me a bottle of water before digging in his jeans pocket. "I take one of these when I feel upset or thrashed, and it really helps take the edge off." He unearths a small blue pill and hands it to me.

"What is it?" I examine the smooth tablet.

"It's a vitamin B pill. It's harmless. I take them all the time."

"Why is there no writing on it?"

"Because I buy them from a naturopath."

I look up at him. "I don't usually take pills if I can avoid it."

Brandon snatches the pill out of my hand. "If you're worried about it, or if you don't trust me, I understand. I'll keep it for myself." He looks put out and annoyed.

I sigh. "Of course I trust you, Brandon. Here, give it to me. If it's just a vitamin pill, I'll take it." I hold out my hand.

He passes the tablet back. "I'll never do anything to hurt you, Soph. I love you. All I'm trying to do is help you feel better."

"I know. And I'm glad you're here." I take the cap off the water and swig some down with the pill.

I slowly pick at the food as Brandon tries to distract me by talking about how great it's going to be at the farmhouse.

"When are you set to move in?" I ask.

"You mean, when are *we* supposed to move in?"

"Yes."

"In just two weeks. Though, it seems like it's too far away. I can't wait for us to wake up every morning together."

I smile. "I can't wait, either." I'm happy that I won't have to be alone with my thoughts for too much longer.

Then I remember that my mom is coming for a week. I guess while she's here, I'll have some time to break the news about Brandon to her.

I'm so glad my father isn't coming. He would have a coronary if he knew I was shacking up with someone he's never met and given his approval on. It'll be much better if my mom breaks the news to him after she flies back to Scotland. She's always had a way to defuse his reactions.

When I've eaten all I can—about half of what he gave me—Brandon takes my plate away and brings it to the kitchen. While he's in the other room, I get up to use the bathroom.

Suddenly, I feel a huge rush up my body to my head. I sit back down and focus on a spot on the wall.

When Brandon walks back into the room, he notices I'm not moving and sits beside me, looking concerned. "Is something wrong?"

"I don't know. I just tried to stand and I got this huge rush."

He laughs. "Oh, that's probably the vitamin pill. Don't worry about it. Just give it a couple of minutes to level out in your body."

He puts his arm around me and starts to hum a sweet melody as I take deep breaths to relax. After a few minutes, I slowly get up, hoping that the rush feeling doesn't come back—it doesn't.

Instead, I'm starting to feel good. Like, really good. My body feels warm and comfortable and all of my heartache and confusion over Tessa is quickly fading. I look at Brandon. "Wow. I feel wonderful."

He laughs. "Yeah, that's a great vitamin B pill. It does wonders for me when I'm stressed."

I smile. "I never knew a vitamin could make me feel so good."

I walk to the bathroom and look in the mirror. My face looks a little fuzzy and my eyes are red, probably from all of the crying I did earlier. I rinse my face and brush out my hair, then walk back to the bedroom.

Brandon is lying with the blankets pulled halfway up his bare chest. As soon as he looks at me, a wave of pure love comes over me. I know I should be mourning Tessa and not thinking about myself, but I can't help it. I have a crazy desire to make love to Brandon right now.

* * *

The soft touch of Brandon's fingers on my face rouses me from a deep sleep. I look over and see him grinning at me. Hoping I wasn't ugly dreaming, I blush with embarrassment and put a hand over my face.

He gently pulls my hand away. "Don't cover that beautiful face."

"Please tell me you weren't watching me sleep," I groan.

"Come here, silly." He pulls me closer.

As soon as my head moves, I feel a searing pain behind my eyes. I put a hand on my forehead. "Wow. That's weird. I have a headache. I never get them."

"It's because of how upset you were yesterday. It'll go away."

"Do you think it could be caused by the pill I took?"

"Vitamin B? That would be highly unlikely."

I try to ignore my pounding head as I run my fingers over his bare chest. "Do you have to work today?"

He nods, then tells me that it shouldn't take too long; he'll be dealing with his new business, and not working in the shop today. "And what about you? What's on your to-do list?"

I shrug. "I guess I should start on the schoolwork I missed this week. Then I'll probably do some cleaning. My mom is a clean freak, and she'll lecture me like mad if things aren't neat and tidy."

"That's right. Your mom is coming. How long will she be here for?"

"About a week. Though, I think she'll be spending a lot of time with Tessa's family while she's here. They're old family friends."

"I can't wait to meet her, even under the circumstances."

"You'll really like her. She can be a lot of fun. However, it's best I spend the first couple of days with her alone, so I can tell her about you before you come over. Otherwise, it may be a little overwhelming, considering the whole Tessa thing."

"Whatever you think is best," he says, kissing my forehead.

* * *

Once my headache fades, I sit in front of my laptop and get busy with my homework. Since Brandon left a couple of hours ago, I've kept myself busy so I don't dwell too much on Tessa. I'm too afraid of getting pulled back into the painful vortex of grief. It doesn't stop her face from flashing through my mind every few minutes.

Brandon calls me at noon to see how I'm doing. What a thoughtful guy. He tells me that I should be dressed and looking pretty at five tonight, so he can take me for dinner at the best Italian restaurant in Abbotsford. I've never been there, as fine dining isn't usually something I can afford on a student's budget.

With a number of hours left until I have to get ready, I grab a bucket from under the sink and fill it halfway with water. To it I add a few capfuls of vinegar—my mom's home cleaning recipe.

Starting in the bathroom, I do a thorough scrub of everything visible. Next, I carry the bucket into my room to clean the window, wipe the dresser down, and dust the lamps.

As I clean, I notice a hair elastic on the floor and pick it up. I open the small drawer on the table beside the bed to put the elastic away, and immediately, my eyes are drawn to a small piece of paper. I recognize Tessa's handwriting.

With a deep sigh, I slide the paper out of the drawer. It's the note Tessa wrote me the night she disappeared. I slowly run my fingers over the words.

I'm so sorry, Tess.

What could I have done differently that night? What could I have done to change what happened?

My eyes fill with tears and I sit down on the bed, clutching the note. She was too damn young to die, especially in such a horrific way. She wanted to change her life and do better. If she had gotten back into school, she could've gone on to be something great, like a doctor or a therapist.

I set the paper on the nightstand and lie down on the bed. Suddenly, I'm not feeling very well, and whatever energy I had earlier is draining fast.

Thankfully, I doze off for quite a while. When I wake, I look out the window and see that night is fast approaching, which means Brandon will be here soon enough.

Flipping through my closet, I can't find anything remotely dressy enough for a dinner date. Finally, I settle on a white t-shirt, blue jeans, and a black blazer.

I'm just finishing my hair when the text comes from Brandon. I quickly pull on my knee-length black boots and head downstairs.

As soon as I see him, all my worries about Tess and my mom coming diminish. I slide in next to him. He kisses me, then takes my hand.

At the restaurant, we sit at a small, white cloth-covered table by a large fireplace. The soft sounds of Italy play through the overhead speakers.

Brandon mentions how he'd love to travel around Europe with me one day. He says that we could visit all of the sites, eat at great cafés, then make love all night. I picture everything he is saying and grin. I'd go anywhere with him.

Chapter Eight

A few days pass. When Brandon isn't working, he's helping me get my unit ready for when my mom arrives.

I'm both excited and worried about her upcoming visit. On one hand, I can't wait to hug her again, but on the other hand, I'm concerned that she won't approve of Brandon. I just hope she's open-minded enough to see the wonderful person behind the rocker vibe and past all his tattoos.

* * *

Last night was the first time I slept alone since the Island. As Mom will be arriving at the Vancouver Airport at 7AM, Brandon decided it would be best if he slept at his place. Still, we spent half the night gabbing on the phone. By the time we finally hung up, there were only a couple of hours remaining until I had to leave for the airport.

Once I'm finally parked and in the terminal, I walk all the way through the expansive airport and stand at the arrivals gate. Now that I'm here, I start to feel like a little child again, seeing her mommy after being away at summer camp.

Droves of travelers file down the escalator—families with overtired children, single people carrying headphones and small pillows, and business passengers carrying briefcases and looking focused. Then, near the back, I see her auburn hair.

When her face comes into view, my heart leaps. She looks beautiful. She's wearing a matching top and bottom tracksuit, and even after the long flight, it looks fresh and new. She always was a classy lady; no one would ever guess that most of her wardrobe was purchased at second-hand stores. It wasn't that she was cheap when it came to shelling out big bucks for clothing, but my father was. I guess she'd rather compromise on her spending than have to listen to my dad bitch about the high cost of things.

Her eyes light up when she sees me, and we both start to cry. Once she's off the escalator, we hug and kiss until a large man asks us to get out of the way.

On the drive back to Abbotsford, Mom gets me caught up on all the family news back in Scotland, including the fact that my father has recently been prescribed blood pressure medication. When we get back to my unit, I help Mom put her stuff away, then we sit and chat for a couple of hours before ordering and sharing a large pizza.

Mom calls Mrs. Waters to tell her she's arrived, then gets up to use the bathroom. While she's gone, I quickly call Brandon and tell him that my mother arrived safely, and we're just relaxing at my place. He tells me he loves me, and that he'll see me tomorrow.

Thankfully, Mom hasn't said one negative word about the cleanliness of my place. Thanks to Brandon helping me, I think we did a pretty good job.

Due to the long flight, Mom is exhausted and ready for bed. Normally I wouldn't be tired for hours, but considering I only had a couple of hours of sleep last night, I'm ready to crash as well. I give Mom my bed while I grab a blanket from the linen closet and make up the couch. Sleeping in Tessa's room feels wrong.

After Mom has gone to sleep, I text Brandon a heart emoji and a sleeping smiley face. He doesn't text me back, likely working late in the shop.

* * *

My back is cramped and there's a crick in my neck. I tossed and turned all night; it was the first time I ever slept on the couch, and it wasn't pleasant.

As soon as I start to make coffee, I hear Mom stirring in the bedroom. A few moments later, she comes out fully dressed, her makeup already done.

"Wow, Mom. You look great. You hit the ground running this morning."

"No, not really. I've been up for over an hour. I was just quiet so I didn't wake you."

I hand her a cup of coffee, but she tells me she doesn't have time to drink it. "I'm going to the Waterses' house in a few minutes."

"Why don't I get dressed fast and drive you?"

She shakes her head. "When I got in last night, I booked an Uber for this morning. I didn't want to take up your time, in case you had classes."

"I really could've taken you, Mom. You don't need to waste your money on drivers when my car is just downstairs."

"It's okay, dear. I'll call you when I'm done with my visit today, and you can come and pick me up."

"Of course, Mom. I'm at your disposal."

She glances at her watch, then hugs me goodbye before grabbing her purse and heading downstairs.

I wait a few moments to make sure she doesn't come back up after forgetting something, then slide my phone out of my pocket and call Brandon.

This time, he answers. "Hey, babe, I was just going to text you. How are you and your mom making out?"

I tell him that she's gone for the whole day.

"Good! Get dressed and I'll be there to pick you up in twenty minutes." He hangs up.

I grin at the thought of seeing him, until I look over at my textbooks. I should really stay home and do my homework, especially since my mother is here. If she asks me how my courses are going, which she will, it's a lot harder to lie to her face than it is over the phone.

I sigh and call Brandon back. As soon as he answers and I hear his voice, my heart sinks. I know he's going to be disappointed.

"Brandon, I know we've only been apart for one night, but it feels like forever. I want to go with you so badly, but I don't think I can. I have homework to do and if my mom finds out I'm behind on my studies, she'll be very upset. I'm so sorry."

He doesn't answer for a moment or two. "Don't be silly," he finally says. "There will be lots of time to catch up on your essays before the semester is over. Plus, you're a smart girl. It's not like you're going to fail. You've just lost your friend, and now your mom is here from Scotland—I think that gives you a bit of a pass on doing homework."

He does have some good points. I may be a bit behind right now, but as soon as Mom leaves and flies back home, I'll just dive into my homework headfirst. I'll get it done long before the semester ends. "Okay. I'll meet you downstairs in twenty minutes."

I smile and sprint to the bathroom to fix myself up.

* * *

He looks so handsome; his hair is styled perfectly and he's wearing a fitted long-sleeved Henley over a pair of dark blue jeans. As soon as I get in the truck, he leans over and gives me the most tender kiss.

My head is spinning pleasantly. "So, where are we going?"

"Furniture shopping."

"Furniture shopping? Really?"

"Well, yeah. The house we're moving into isn't furnished, and I want you to be a part of every decision regarding what goes in it."

"That's really sweet, but if the furniture is going to be ours, shouldn't I be paying half?" I feel a spike of panic, knowing there's no way I can afford furniture on a student's budget.

"You're a bit of a worrier, aren't you?" He winks at me.

"I just want things to be fair."

"Why don't we just enjoy the day, and worry about it some other time."

* * *

I soon learn how great Brandon is at haggling for a deal.

We've picked out a leather sofa and a matching La-Z-Boy chair, as well as a gorgeous wall unit, and he talked the guy down thirty percent.

Brandon then grabs my hand and leads me to the other side of the store, where the bedroom sets are sold. He looks at three or four bed displays, then has me lie back on each mattress. With the salesclerk ogling us, I feel a little awkward. Brandon picks up on my nervousness and tries to break the tension; on the last bed he throws himself on top of me and kisses me. Horrified and embarrassed, I laugh nervously and try to get up, but he keeps trying to kiss me.

"Brandon!" I whisper through my laughter. "Please get off me. She's watching us."

He stops, then turns his head to the clerk. "I think we'll take this one."

I quickly maneuver off the bed and finger-brush my now messed-up hair.

At the till, he hands over a gold credit card and arranges a time to pick the furniture up.

When we're walking out of the store, I look over at him. "You are insane. I thought that woman was going to lose it on us."

He laughs. "Honey, she doesn't give a damn what people do, as long as they buy something."

I shake my head and smile as we get into the truck.

We go for lunch at a small Korean Bar-B-Que joint and talk about the new house. He mentions how it'll be great going to bed together every night and waking up beside each other every morning. The thought of being with him on a permanent basis feels like a dream. Just a few months ago, I never would've imagined meeting a guy as perfect as him, let alone moving into a house with him. And after such a short time…it all feels so surreal.

I just hope my parents don't go too crazy when they hear about our impromptu plan. I guess it'll all depend on how the first meeting goes between my mom and Brandon. I pray she likes him.

Back at the entrance of my place, we spend a long time kissing and petting before Brandon has to get back to work. Apparently he'd told his boss that he was running errands so he could buy some time with me.

I hop out of the truck and stand on the path, feeling sad as he pulls away. I have to have a talk with Mom soon and tell her about my new boyfriend. Otherwise, I'll barely get to see him.

* * *

I'm just opening my textbooks when my mom calls for me to pick her up.

As soon as I pull up to the house, my mom opens the door and walks to the car. When she gets in, I can see by the redness of her eyes that she's been crying.

"Are you okay, Mom?" I put my hand on her leg.

She nods and pulls out a handkerchief to wipe her nose. "I'm not the one who lost a daughter, of course. I'm okay."

"I know. I feel so bad for Tessa's parents."

"They are dealing with it the best they can. And at least they have each other."

"Was there any new information about Tessa's death?"

"Not really. Just that she was strangled, and there were a bunch of pills found in her stomach."

"Pills? Really?"

"Why does that surprise you? You knew she was into partying."

"I know. But she really wanted to change her life around. She sounded so sincere when she talked about giving up her old ways."

My mom looks at me and tilts her head, as if to say *get real*. "I don't know if that girl had it in her to straighten out her life. She was drawn to the wild side from a very young age."

"I guess you're right," I say, even though I'm finding it hard to believe that Tess could be so adamant about changing one minute, then go out and do drugs the next.

My mom starts to cry again and grabs onto my hand. "I'm just relieved that you're on a good path. That instead of focusing on parties and drugs, you're focussed on school. I guess your father and I were just lucky that way."

I glance over at her and smile, though guilt courses through me. This definitely isn't the time to bring up Brandon.

Once we're back at my unit, Mom goes into the bedroom and calls Dad while I sit on the sofa and start on homework. It'll cheer her up to see me hitting the books.

After about an hour, my mom pokes her head out. "I'm trying to tell your father the correct name of the pills that were found in Tessa's stomach. Is it Fedrasyl or Fentanyl?

"I think it's Fentanyl, Mom."

"Okay. Thank you." She closes the bedroom door.

I go back to my essay, but then what my mother said hits me. *Tessa had Fentanyl in her system?*

That's crazy. Even for Tessa. She knew about the dangers of that drug. There are always news bulletins stating how many people die from using it. I remember her taking drugs to make her feel up and drugs to make her sleepy, but never did I hear her talk about Fentanyl. I would've remembered that.

After another half hour passes, Mom comes out of the bedroom and suggests I order us a pizza. "You must be starving. You've been doing your schoolwork all day, kiddo. As proud of you as I am, you still need to take time from studying to eat."

I'm not the least bit hungry, not after eating out with Brandon, but I can't tell her that. Not yet.

"Sure Mom. I'll call right away."

* * *

We spend the rest of the afternoon and evening hanging out. After our food, I lie on one side of the couch while she lies on the other, and we watch TV. It feels good to be so close to her again. My parents were all I had growing up, but I can't help feeling somewhat changed since they moved away. I'm not sure if it's because I've been in a grown-up relationship with Brandon, or because I've been living on my own, but I don't feel like a kid anymore.

When the movie we've been watching ends, Mom tells me that she's tired. She gives me a big hug and a kiss, then says good night. I wait until the bedroom door closes before quietly calling Brandon.

He answers on the first ring. "Hello, beautiful. How was your day?"

I tell him how upset my mother was when I picked her up, and that she learned Tessa had ingested Fentanyl before she died.

"That's a heavy drug," he says. "You'd think she'd know better than to mess around with that crap."

"I really did think she knew better." I pause. "I still kind of do."

"I'm confused. If they found pills in her system, it's kind of obvious she took them."

"I know. I haven't figured that part out yet. But something tells me there's more to the story that's yet to be told."

He chuckles. "Listen to you. You're a regular Nancy Drew."

"Not quite. I just really can't see her willingly taking Fentanyl. Maybe other stuff less potent, but not a heavy drug like that."

"Maybe you're right, sweetie. I guess you'll have to wait and see if more information comes out about the events leading up to her death."

"Yeah, that's the frustrating part."

146

"Have the police mentioned anything about a suspect, or are they still searching?"

"Mom didn't say anything about that, so they probably don't have anyone in custody yet."

"Don't worry. I'm sure whoever did this will be caught."

"I hope you're right."

"Well, just to get your mind off the subject, I have some great news."

"Good. I could use some right now."

He tells me he'll be picking up the new furniture in the morning, and that the owner of the farmhouse has agreed to let us move in a week early.

"That's so great! I can't wait to see the place. I just hope it's not too far from campus."

"It shouldn't be too far. Plus, when the snow comes, I can drive you in my truck."

I smile. "You've got all the bases covered, don't you?"

"I always do."

We talk for a while longer, until I tell him I should get back to studying. He tells me he loves me, then asks when he can meet my mother.

The subject immediately makes me anxious. "I haven't brought you up to her yet. She was far too upset when she came back from Tessa's parents' place. I'll try and talk to her tomorrow, I promise."

Brandon sounds a bit hurt when he answers. "It sucks that I'm supposed to be an important person in your life now, but your parents don't even know about me yet. I feel like your dirty little secret."

"I'm sorry. And I promise I will talk to her in the morning. I want her to know all about you."

"Okay. Good. I hope she takes the news well."

Yeah, me too.

* * *

Ominous clouds fill the morning sky, and it's only a matter of time before rain pours down.

I'm bummed that the weather isn't behaving while my mom is here. Then again, she's used to Scotland, so I guess it's not too much of an adjustment.

Once Mom is up and we've both had our first cup of coffee, we discuss what we should do today. Mrs. Waters is busy dealing with the funeral home and making burial arrangements, so she won't be available to visit with Mom until tomorrow sometime. So, the day is ours. Mom decides that she wants to shop for food items she can't get in Scotland, so after we're dressed, we head to the mall.

We browse a few clothing stores before heading to the grocery store. Mom fills the cart with Kraft Dinner—my father's favorite lunch—maple candies and syrup, and boxes of different cereals. I laugh when we go through the check-out—we look like junk food junkies.

On the way back home, I turn on the radio. "On the Road Again" by Canned Heat comes on. I turn up the volume and we sing along until we arrive at campus. Our arms full, we get to the unit and set the bounty of goodies on the floor.

I look down at the overstuffed bags. "Mom. How are you going to pack all of this into your suitcase?"

"With great skill," she giggles.

Mom puts the kettle on to make a pot of tea, and I flop out on the sofa and watch her. I'm taking mental pictures of her so that when she returns to Scotland, I can replay them in my mind.

She catches me looking. "What are you staring at, kid? Don't you have some homework to do or something?"

"I guess so." I grab my textbooks from the side table.

As I navigate through my books, Mom sets a cup of tea in front of me and says she's going to the bedroom to make some calls. I immerse myself in homework and before I know it, three hours have passed.

I get up, stretch my legs, and look out the window. I wonder what Brandon is doing right now. Is he thinking about me?

Then, I remember my promise. I gave my word that I would tell my mom about him, and maybe set up a time when he can come over to meet her.

A hard lump forms in my throat at the thought. I haven't introduced either of my parents to a guy since I was in high school, and I'm horrified at the thought of doing so now, regardless of the fact that I'm twenty-three.

I wash up my tea mug and am just putting it back in the cupboard when Mom walks out of the bedroom. "Have your eyes crossed from studying yet?"

I chuckle. "Nah. I'm pretty used to it."

"Any ideas about what we should do for dinner? I guess we kind of missed lunch."

"I'll see if I can find a good place on the internet. Since you and Dad moved away, there have been quite a few new restaurants opened here."

Should I talk to her about my new boyfriend before or after dinner? I don't want to ruin her appetite if she finds the topic stressful, but I can't go back on my word to Brandon, either. I guess there's no perfect time.

I take a deep breath and ask her to sit beside me on the couch. "I have to tell you something." I struggle to keep eye-contact.

"It isn't stressful news, is it? I just don't know if I could handle any more bad news right now."

I shake my head. "Well, I don't think it's bad news. Not to me."

"Okay, then, good. What is it?"

"I...I met a guy."

She stares at me for a few long moments. "Oh. Okay. Is he a student?

"No. He's older, and he works at an auto body shop here in Abbotsford. He's just starting his own business."

"If he's not a student, where did you meet him?"

I definitely can't tell the truth about meeting Brandon at a party. "I met him through a friend," I say, only partially lying.

"And he has family here?"

"No. His father passed away and his mother lives out East."

She considers this for a few beats. "This new relationship hasn't diverted you from your studies, has it?"

"Of course not. He's been very supportive of my studies."

"I see. Well, I guess it was inevitable that you'd meet someone. Your father and I just hoped it would happen after you were finished at university."

"I know. And I know your concerns. But, Mom, if you will just meet him, all of your concerns will be gone. He's incredible, really!"

"Look at your face light up when you talk about him. You sound like you're in love."

"I think I am, Mom. I've never met anyone like him."

She puts her arm around me and pulls me close. "I know you have a good head on your shoulders. You probably get that from my side of the family." We laugh. "If you say he's a good guy, and he makes you happy, I'll meet him. What's his name?"

"Brandon."

"That's a ridiculous name."

"Mom!"

"Just kidding."

We order two curry dishes from a local restaurant. After eating, we sit on the couch and I call Brandon. I feel awkward calling my boyfriend in front of my mom, but now that she knows about him, there's no point in waiting until she's out of the room to talk to him anymore.

"Hi. It's me. How was your day?"

Brandon tells me he's been buying dishes and things for the new house. Thankfully, I don't have him on speaker phone. I'm not sure she could handle hearing that I'm planning on moving in with him right away. I'll have to break that news to her slowly.

"So, I told my mom about you. I think it would be great for you two to meet."

"Really? That's great. Can I come over now?"

I cover the receiver. "Mom. Brandon really wants to meet you. Do you mind if he comes over tonight?"

She shrugs. "I guess so. But I don't want a long visit. I've got to get up early and go to the Waterses' house tomorrow morning."

I smile and mouth *thank you* to her. "Sure, come over," I say to Brandon.

As soon as the call ends, I jet to the bathroom to put on makeup and fix my hair. My mom walks in just as I'm plugging in my curling iron. "My goodness, this fella has you in a tizzy."

"No. I just don't want to look like I've been pulled through a knothole backwards."

Mom laughs. "You must really be smitten by this guy."

I grin. "Wait until you see him. You'll understand."

Once I'm finished in the washroom, I quickly change into fresh tights and a matching top. Just as I'm walking out of the bedroom, there are a couple hard raps on the door.

I answer the door to Brandon standing in front of me. He'd dressed respectably in jeans and a dress shirt, and he's carrying a fresh bouquet of flowers.

I smile. "Are those for me?"

He shakes his head. "Nope. I brought them for your mom."

As soon as he walks into the living room, my mom gets up from the sofa and walks over to him. "Hi. I'm Sophie's mom."

"Wow. It's obvious where your daughter gets her good looks from.' He passes her the bouquet. "These are for you."

"They're lovely. Thank you, Brandon."

When Mom has finished putting the flowers in a vase, Brandon and I sit on the sofa and mom pulls a chair over and sits in front of us.

"So," she begins. "Sophie tells me you're in the car business."

Brandon nods. "Yes. I work at an auto body shop downtown."

"I see. And you're planning on starting your own outfit?"

"I am. I'm in the process of getting everything together now."

"Where do you live?"

I look at my mom's eyes. She's studying him closely as he answers, sizing him up. The discussion is starting to seem more like an inquisition than a conversation.

Trying to change the energy in the room, I interrupt, "Hey, Mom. Why don't you tell Brandon and me about your new place in Scotland? Is it close to town? Does Dad love it?"

"Slow down, Sophie. Why are you talking so fast?"

"I'm not talking fast, Mom. I'm just interested, and I know Brandon probably is, too."

"Your father and I already told you about the new place, but I'll tell you again if you're interested."

She talks about how their new condo is located by a pretty river, and how their yard is small but has a big enough garden to feed them throughout the summer. I've heard all this before, just after they moved there, but at least she's not focussing on giving Brandon the fifth degree anymore.

When she's finished describing their home and the area, I ask her and Brandon if they would like something to drink. Brandon declines and says that he should be going, as he has to be up super early. I offer to walk him to the foyer downstairs, and Mom looks at him and says a brief goodbye.

Outside in the hallway, Brandon looks at me and exhales hard. "Wow. That was a bit intense. She was just starting to build up steam with all those questions."

"I know. I am so sorry. She's a nice person, she's just a little paranoid about me dating, especially after what just happened to Tessa. I think you'd really like her if you met her in different circumstances."

He leans over and kisses me. "As long as you're into me, I don't care about who likes me or who doesn't."

"Good." I wrap my arms around him.

After a long, sensual kiss, I tell him I'll text him after Mom goes to bed.

When I walk back into the unit, Mom is making a pot of tea. As I walk past her on my way to the sofa, she glances up at me. I don't say a word to her until she carries the tea over and sets a mug in front of me.

"Well?" I say.

"Well, what?"

"You know what I'm talking about, Mom. What did you think about Brandon?"

"Can't we talk about something else?"

"Why?"

"I don't want you to get upset."

"What are you talking about? Why would I get upset?"

"Because you really want me to like him. I can tell."

"And you don't?"

"Not remotely."

I sit up straight and look at her with disbelief. "How can you say that? He was only here for a half hour. That's not giving him much of a chance. You don't even know him."

"I know people, Sophie. I'm a lot older than you. I've been alive for a long time. I've met a lot of people in my life, and I can tell a bad egg when I see one."

I'm feeling angry now. "That's ridiculous."

"See? Now you're upset with me for telling the truth."

"I'm upset with you because I think you're being narrow-minded."

"I saw in his eyes, Sophie. He's a manipulator and a liar. I've always been able to tell the character of someone by looking into their eyes. Your new boyfriend doesn't fool me."

I shake my head and sigh. "You're right, Mom. We shouldn't talk about this."

* * *

After a restless night of tossing and turning, and mulling over my mother's unfair judgment of Brandon, I get up and have a shower.

Last night was unbearable; Mom and I watched TV for a couple of hours and barely spoke a word to one another. Once she went to bed, I texted Brandon and apologized again for the way she interrogated him.

"It's okay babe, he texted. *Don't sweat it."*

I'm glad that you don't seem easily offended. Once Mom gets to know you, she'll love you as much as I do.

There was a joking tone to his next text. *Does that mean I have to meet with her again?*

Thankfully, Mom and I will be apart for most of the day, as I'll soon be dropping her off at Tessa's parents. Maybe this evening, when I pick her up, she'll have changed her thinking about my boyfriend.

Mr. Waters ended up giving Mom a ride to their place, which gave me a head start on my homework. Finally, I'm beginning to see the light at the end of the tunnel, and I only have a couple more essays to wrap up before I'm on par again.

I take a break at around 11AM. Just then, Brandon calls to tell me that he is driving out to the new place, and wants me to come along. He promises not to keep me very long, since he has to be back at work in the afternoon. I get dressed and wait for him downstairs in the lobby.

As soon as I see him, I forget about the tension between Mom and me, and about the rest of the homework I need to do.

We drive quite a ways out of town, then pass a rickety old motel and turn down a bumpy dirt road toward the mountains.

"Wow. This place is a long way out of town, isn't it?" I say, looking out the window.

Brandon puts his hand on my leg. "Just think of the privacy we'll have."

Finally, we pull up a long driveway with an old washing machine on one side and a rusty red mailbox on the other. Ahead is a barn that looks like it'd blow over in a strong wind. Once we drive around the barn,

Brandon stops the truck in front of an old run-down house.

It's not as big as I thought it would be. It's narrow, with two storeys, and looks extremely unsafe.

Brandon grins. "Well, what do you think?"

For a moment I think he's joking, and has driven me to the wrong property to see if he can freak me out. Then again, if this really is the place, I don't want to insult him by saying anything negative. I don't meet his eye when I answer. "Wow, it's definitely not what I was expecting."

"Wait until you see the inside. It's great."

When he shuts off the truck and opens his door, my heart sinks. He's not joking. This really is the place.

He tells me to watch my step and he leads me up the crooked front stairs. I'm almost surprised when he produces a key for the front door. Who would care about locking the door to this broken-down shack?

The hinges creak when he pushes the door open, and we walk inside. My eyes scan the floors as I walk. If I see a mouse, Brandon is going to be piggy backing me out of here.

"Well, what do you think?" he asks again.

I think I should get a tetanus shot before I move in. "It's definitely got character," I say, trying to be positive.

"Exactly." His tone is excited. "I mean look at how cool it is. Who wouldn't want to live here?"

I don't know, someone with taste and twenty-twenty vision? "You mentioned before that we'll have the upstairs, and your friends will be living on the main floor?"

"Yeah, that's right."

Good. It'll be harder for the mice to navigate the stairs.

"Do you want to go upstairs and have a look?" He grabs my hand and leads me up the narrow stairwell.

As I walk behind him, I'm careful not to touch the dusty railing or brush up against the paint peeled walls. "So, how did you find this gem?"

"By pure luck. I know a guy who knows the owner of this place. He's the one that put in a good word for me."

If he referred you to this place, I'm not so sure he was a friend.

Once upstairs, Brandon leads me through three different rooms that could pass for pantries. In the last room, he walks me across the floor to the small window. "Would you look at this beautiful view?"

Granted, it's a pretty picture of the mountains, but as soon as you look down, all you notice are the rusted cars and

160

discarded pieces of what looks like farming equipment. "It's definitely a unique property."

"I know! And I can't wait to put our new furniture in here. "

The unit I live in on campus is small, and I never really thought it was that extraordinary…until now. Compared to this place, it's a suite at the Hilton.

Brandon leans in and kisses me softly. I kiss him back, and quickly things start to heat up.

He slides his cold hands up my shirt. "It's been days since we made love."

The chill of his hands on my warm skin makes my body tense, and I let out a squeal. "What? You want to do it now? Here?"

He smiles. "If I don't have you now, I'll explode."

"Brandon, I want to do it as badly as you do, but there's no bed. Besides, it's freezing cold in here."

"We'll warm up fast. And we don't need a bed. You can just slide your jeans down and put your hands on the wall."

I glance at the dirty, water-stained wall behind me and shake my head. "Can't we make love somewhere else?"

All of a sudden, he seems distant. His eyes squint and he looks almost angry. "You don't like it here, do you?" He pushes away and turns his back to me.

I put my hand on his shoulder. "That's not it at all," I lie. "It just needs a good cleaning, that's all. I think it's great, really I do."

He slowly turns to face me. "You know, I got this place for us, so we can be together. I know it's not the Ritz Carlton, but I thought it wouldn't matter where we live, as long as we're together."

"That's so true." I kiss him on the cheek. "Please don't be upset with me."

Slowly, a grin starts to form. "How can I stay mad at you?"

* * *

On the ride back to Abbotsford, I slide next to him and put my head on his shoulder. He talks about how his boss is really getting on his nerves and he can't wait until his own business is up and running. Then I talk about my mother and the tension between us. "It's so bad, I couldn't sleep very well."

"You need your sleep, Sophie. It's very important, especially when you're in school."

"I know. But Mom leaves in two days. If I can make it until then, I can sleep when she leaves."

"You'll be a zombie by then." He glances at me. "I actually have something that'll help you get rest without making you feel whacked out."

"More Vitamin B pills?"

"No. These ones are to help mellow you out, so you can get some rest."

"Melatonin?"

"No. They're better, but just as harmless."

"Okay. If you say they're safe, then I trust you."

He leans over me and opens the glove compartment, from which he pulls out a small baggy of white pills. "Take a few out of the bag and put them in your pocket."

After I do what he says, I ask him what the pills are called. He says he got them from his naturopath, and he can't remember what they're called.

* * *

Mom hasn't said much to me since she got back to my place. I try to break the ice, but nothing seems to change the look of worry on her face. Finally, I give up and do homework for the rest of the evening. Mom goes to the bedroom and closes the door.

When my eyes get blurry from hours of studying, I put my books away and try to relax on the couch, but my mind is focused on the tension between Mom and me. I feel both hurt and angry about her reaction to Brandon. If she'd be more open-minded and let him in, I know she'd be crazy about him, but she's being stubborn and judgemental and won't even try. All of this bad energy is ruining our visit. She's leaving soon, and who knows when we'll see each other again.

I toss and turn for a while before I remember the tablets that Brandon gave me earlier. I pull them out of my jeans pocket and swallow one down with a glass of water.

* * *

"Sophie. Wake up!"

When I open my eyes, everything is blurry. "What, Mom? Are you okay?"

"What's wrong with you? Why did it take so long for you to wake up?"

When I grab onto the back of the couch and pull myself up, the room spins and I feel like I'm going to throw up. "I'm fine."

"Why are you still in your street clothes?"

"Mom. Please lower your voice and calm down. I'm okay. I was studying late and I guess I just fell asleep in my clothes."

She takes a seat in front of me and her face starts coming into focus. She leans closer. "Did you take something, Sophie?"

"Don't be silly, Mom. You know I hate drugs. What would I have taken?"

164

"You seem pretty groggy and out of it to be only tired."

"You're just being paranoid because of the whole Tessa thing."

"I hope you're right. It would destroy me if you were taking drugs."

I look over at the clock on the microwave. It's 4AM. "Mom, why are you up so early?"

She tells me that she got up to use the washroom. "When I saw you on the couch without my pajamas on and sprawled out in a weird position, I got scared. Especially when you didn't wake up right away."

Looking at her face, I feel my frustration and anger toward her disappear. Her face is creased with worry.

We sit and talk until she's satisfied that I'm okay. Then I give her a heartfelt hug and she goes back to the bedroom.

When I stand to change into my pajamas, I just about fall over. Whatever Brandon gave me was way too strong. I can't imagine that a pill from a naturopath could be so powerful.

By the time morning breaks, my head feels clearer and the dizziness has passed. Mom makes breakfast as I have a cool shower to help me wake up. After I get dressed, I go into the front room to find two plates of microwaved egg muffins on the coffee table. I sit beside my mother on the couch and put the plate on my lap. "Thanks for making this for me, Mom."

"How are you feeling?"

"Fine. I got a lot of sleep."

She gives me a long look. "I leave tomorrow, Sophie."

I sigh. "I know."

"It's important for me to know that you'll be okay here alone."

"Mom, there are so many other students in this building."

"I didn't mean alone in the unit. I meant alone in Canada, without your father and me."

"Oh. Don't worry. I'm okay."

"I was talking to your father and told him about your new boyfriend. He seems to think that you might fare better living with us in Scotland. You wouldn't be able to apply to the university right away, as you'd be coming in between semesters, but you could always—"

"What? I'm not going to Scotland."

"I just think you should think about it, Sophie. Keep an open mind."

"Keep an open mind? Like you did with Brandon?"

"I do not want to fight with you. I just wanted you to know that there are options open to you. Besides, if you did come to Scotland for school, even for a year, your friend would still be here if you decided to come back."

I put my plate back on the coffee table. "My life is here, Mom, and I'm going to stay in Abbotsford with my boyfriend. In fact, we'll be moving in together very soon."

As soon as the words leave my lips, I regret saying them.

Mom immediately starts to cry, and I know I've gone too far. She leaves tomorrow, and there's no way I'm going to be able to talk her down before she gets on the plane. Why did I have to tell her about the move? I feel like a horrible daughter.

After spending a couple of hours in the bedroom and refusing to talk to me, Mom calls Mr. Waters and has him pick her up. She doesn't come back until bedtime, and as soon as she walks through the door, she heads to the bedroom to call my father.

I set my clock for 5AM, as I need to have her at the airport a couple of hours before her plane leaves.

As I lie on the couch, my heart feels heavy. I wonder how long it will be before she returns to Canada. Tears roll down my cheeks as I reach into my pocket and take half of the other pill Brandon gave me.

I'm sure it won't hit me as hard, considering I'm only taking half the dosage. I try to call Brandon, but there's no answer. It sure would make me feel a lot better if I could hear his voice right now.

* * *

Thankfully, I'm not dizzy and my vision isn't blurred when the alarm wakes me. I get up and rap on the bedroom door, telling my mom it's time to get up. She doesn't say anything, but after a few minutes I can hear her milling about.

I make a quick tea and put my shoes on. Mom opens the bedroom door and walks out, pulling her luggage.

"Did you fit all the food in there?" I ask.

"Yes, though I think I crushed one of the boxes of cereal."

I laugh.

On the way to the airport, I try everything I can think of to provoke conversation. Nothing works. When we turn into the airport, I'm just about to drive into the underground parking area when Mom says I can just let her off at the loading area of the departures entrance.

"Don't you want me to park and come in with you?"

She shakes her head. "I told your father I'd call him when I got to the airport. Besides, I'll probably go straight to baggage check, then wait at the gate. You won't be able to come with me there."

I exhale loudly, feeling hurt. "Okay, Mom. It's your call. I'll just drop you off."

I drive up to the loading area and put my four-ways on, then get out and pull her suitcase out of the trunk. As I set the case on its wheels and pass her the handle, she finally makes eye contact with me.

"I love you, Sophie. You know I do. But I cannot lie to you and say I like this Brandon fella you're going with. He's dangerous, and I don't trust him. Now you tell me you're moving in with him, and you don't know the impact that has had. You are my only child, and I will love you until my last breath, but don't ask me to be okay with your current choices. Your father feels the same way."

I look at the ground, take a deep breath, then look back at her. "I don't want to argue, Mom. I just want you to know that I love you very much and I'm sorry if you're disappointed with me. Please tell Dad that I miss him and love him." Then, I lean in and hug her.

"Take care of yourself, Sophie. Make good choices and be strong."

As she walks into the airport, dragging her suitcase, I want to run after her and promise I won't see Brandon again, just to ease her worries, but I can't. I love him too much.

Chapter Nine

For the rest of the morning, I try to finish my homework, but can't. I'm riddled with guilt that my mother left feeling so upset. At least I'll be able to see Brandon tonight, which will take my mind off my guilty conscience. Giving up on homework, I decide to tidy up my unit to pass the time.

With an armful of bedding, I walk down to the laundry room. I'm just opening the washing machine when I hear someone walk into the small room behind me. When I turn to look, I recognize the girl from my floor. She lives with two or three other students, and all of them are partiers. Often, I've had to knock on their door and tell them to keep it down so I could study.

Ignoring her, I load the washer and close the lid. Just as I go to leave, the girl stops me. "You're Sophie, right?"

I nod.

"I am so sorry about Tessa. The news of what happened to her was in this morning's paper. It's very sad."

Her words seem heartfelt, but with the pain I'm already feeling over the tiff with my mom, talking about Tessa will really push me over the edge right now.

I try to be brief but sincere. "Yes, it was a tragic thing. She will be missed."

Then, as I try to walk past her, she grabs me and gives me an awkward hug, patting me a couple of times on my back.

"Thanks." I smile before making a quick getaway.

As I trudge back up to my room, my head filled with thoughts of how Tessa's death will impact life on campus for me from here on out, I start to feel defeated. Instead of finishing my cleaning, I lie down on the sofa and close my eyes.

I wake to the sound of hard rapping on the door. I quickly get to my feet and straighten myself out before answering. It's the same girl from the laundry room.

"I hope you don't mind, but I waited for two hours to use the washing machine and you didn't come back. So, I dried your bedding and folded it." She hands me my linens.

"Wow. Thank you. I'm sorry, I must've nodded off."

"Don't worry. It's completely understandable, considering what you're dealing with right now."

Oh great, it's already started. Soon, I'll be treated as a victim by everyone.

I thank her for her kindness, then close the door. As I make the bed, I think about how moving in with Brandon is probably the best thing, regardless that I'll be moving into that run-down shack. At least I won't be here and the focus of everyone's pity.

Brandon calls just after dinner. He's coming over to spend the night. I can't wait to be immersed in him, and to not worry about everything else.

I make sure I look good for him, with my hair down and wearing a small sheath nightie. From the way he behaved the last time I saw him, I'm sure the first place he'll want to take me is the bedroom.

He shows up with a grin from ear to ear. As predicted, he almost immediately leads me into the bedroom. It feels so good to be enwrapped with him. Both of us are engrossed with each other as the rest of the world falls away.

We make love well into the night, only stopping long enough to take sips of water. When we're all out of steam, he puts his arms around me and I nestle into his strong chest. I smile and exhale all of my tension. This is heaven, and it's all that matters right now—him and me.

In the morning, Brandon gets up early and kisses me goodbye. I find myself following him to the front door for one more kiss until I see him tonight. As soon as he's gone, I miss him.

I know one thing for sure—I'm completely addicted to him.

* * *

Over the next two days, I pack up my unit in between classes and schoolwork. I box up a number of items and write *free stuff* on the box sides, then leave them in the hall. Other than duplicates of dishes and extra towels, I don't have too much stuff. I was never a clothes horse, so packing up my closet will be easy.

On the second day, Brandon calls at 8PM to say we can start moving in tomorrow. Even though I'm a bit nervous about leaving the sanctity of my unit, I realize that because of Tessa's death being plastered all over the media, my once peaceful place has changed forever. I will never be able to walk the hall and not have someone give me a look of sympathy or, worse, speak to me about Tessa. I can't handle that. I'm too much of a loner to be thrust into the pity position. It's hard enough that my professors all took the time to give me their condolences before prying for any further information I may know about Tessa's case.

Unfortunately, I haven't heard from Mom since she left. But I don't keep trying to reach her. She needs time to digest the news about Brandon, and us moving in together. I can only imagine the impact my news has had on my father, who's even less open-minded than Mom. My guess is that he's needing a few more drinks a night to ease his nerves.

* * *

It's raining like hell out; it figures that today would be the day Brandon is moving me out of the unit. By the time we get all of my boxes to the new place, we're both soaking wet.

It looks a lot different here now that the furniture has been delivered. It's obvious that Brandon put a lot of effort into arranging everything. Unlike the first time I was here, now the place kind of has a homey feel to it.

Brandon tells me that I should put my pots and pans away while he sets up the bathroom. I walk down the stairs and am just bending to grab the box of dishes when the front door swings open, and Ryder and Sylvie walk in.

Immediately my stomach clenches and I tense up. I wish Brandon was downstairs with me right now.

"Hey, roomie." Ryder walks around me.

I nod and pick up the box, then walk down the narrow hallway to the kitchen. I can hear Sylvie and Ryder as they move things in their room with the door open. I start unloading the dishes and setting them on the counter.

Upon opening a cupboard, I scream and jump backward. There's a dead mouse lying on its side, its face toward me.

Sylvie comes into the kitchen with a snarl on her face. "Why the hell are you screaming?" She looks at the mouse, then back at me. "Are you serious? A little mouse freaks you out this badly? You've got a lot to learn about farm living."

I say nothing as she reaches into the cupboard and, with bare hands, grabs the rodent by the tail and walks to the door, tossing the body outside.

I grab paper towel and wet it, then wipe out the shelf before putting my dishes away. Once I'm done, I head upstairs.

Brandon is just putting up a shower curtain when I walk into the bathroom. "There was a dead mouse in the cupboard. It nearly scared me to death."

He snickers, then tells me mice are frequent visitors in older homes, especially in the middle of a large field. "We're trespassers in their home. But don't worry, you'll get used to them."

I don't want to get used to them. And even if Sylvie does insult me, if I see a live mouse anywhere near me, I'll lose my mind.

The sound of footsteps gets louder, until Ryder appears at the bathroom entrance. "Should I install the cameras now?" he asks Brandon.

Brandon nods and Ryder walks away.

"Why do we need cameras here?" I ask.

"Because we'll be bringing all of the car parts out here, and security is a must. There are always low-lifes around that would love to steal whatever they can get their hands on."

I walk into the bedroom and start unpacking my clothes and putting hangers on them. Then I slowly open the closet door, ready to run if any critters jump out at me. After I've shone my phone light in every corner, I grab my clothes and hang them on the bar.

Brandon walks in and smiles. "This is going to be the best, you and me living together."

"And Sylvie and Ryder. Don't forget them." My voice gives away my lack of enthusiasm.

"Yes, but they'll be downstairs, and other than when we need to make meals, we'll be up here in our own little world." He picks me up and lies on the bed with me. "You know what we should do?"

"What?"

"Break the bed in. What do you think?"

"Now? We're not even unpacked yet."

"No. Later on, when I get back."

"What do you mean? You're leaving already?"

"I have no choice. I've got to go to town and pick some stuff up. I won't be very long."

"Can I go with you?"

"Not this time, beautiful. You'd just be in the way."

"Can you at least drop me off at my car? It's still on campus."

"Tomorrow." He kisses me on the cheek.

* * *

Over the next week, and after many mouse sightings, we finally have the top floor livable. Thankfully, Sylvie stays in her room most of the time, making it not so unbearable when I have to go into the kitchen to make food.

Brandon and Ryder have been spending most of the days and part of the nights doing stuff in the barn. I went out there once to bring Brandon a sandwich, and he must've heard me approaching because he met me at the door, took the sandwich, then closed the door before I could step foot inside. Later, he explained that the barn isn't the best place for me because of all of the sharp car parts and dangerous machinery. It was his way of telling me that the barn is off-limits.

My studies have been waning ever since I moved out here. I've also not been making it to all of my classes. Brandon always has a list of things for me to do in the daytime. I told him that I can't let myself get too far behind, or I risk getting kicked out. He just smiled and said that no matter how many days I skip, I'll still ace the courses.

He obviously has no clue how a university works. If I don't produce a doctor's note after the second missed class, I could be in big trouble. Brandon sloughs off my comments like they're no big deal.

I half-thought I'd be hearing from my mom by now. However, I've gotten no texts or emails at all. I wrote her a few days ago, but so far she hasn't bothered to reply. I only hope the reason she's not writing is that she's still disappointed in me, and not because something is wrong with her or my dad.

* * *

The morning wind rattles the single-paned window. I roll over and wrap my arms around Brandon's warm chest. His eyes slowly open and he smiles at me. After a few moments of snuggling with him, I look at the clock beside the bed. It's 7AM, and I have a class at 8:30.

I sit up and give Brandon a kiss on the cheek before heading to the bathroom for a quick shower. Just as I'm lathering soap on my body, Brandon walks into the bathroom. I quickly rinse off and ask him to hand me a towel. When I step out of the shower, he's wiping the steam off of the mirror. "Hey, beautiful, what are your plans today?"

"I've got to get to school. I've used up all of my excuses, so if I don't make it there today, I'll have to cough up a lung or something."

"They aren't going to kick you out of university, Sophie. You're too smart."

"Thanks, but they don't really see it that way. If I want to graduate, I have to attend my classes and do the work. That's the bottom line."

He sighs. "That's a drag."

"Why?"

"Because I have to go to Chilliwack with Ryder this morning on business, and at the same time, someone is coming here in an hour to pick up an important parcel."

"Can't you just put off your trip to Chilliwack?"

"No. If I do that, the customer we're meeting with will take his business somewhere else. We need this guy's business badly."

"Brandon, I honestly can't miss another class. There's no way. I'm on very thin ice to begin with."

"You would only have to stay here for an hour, tops. Then you could make it in time for your other classes."

"But I'd still have to blow off my first class."

"I know." He reaches out and touches my cheek. "But you'd be helping me get my business going, which will eventually make it so I don't have to work so much and be away from you." His eyes are desperate and sincere. "I'm doing everything for us. Don't you see that?"

I sigh. "I guess I could write the professor now and tell her I'm having trouble getting to class. She'll want to know why later, but it may buy me some time."

Brandon smiles. "That's my girl." He kisses me on the forehead. "I'll leave the box in the kitchen. Dan, a guy I know, should be by soon to grab it. He'll give you a sealed envelope for me. Just put it in my top dresser drawer."

* * *

After emailing my prof and telling her I won't be attending this morning's class, I tidy up the bedroom and head downstairs to make some toast. I look at the counter and see a box, similar in size to a shoebox.

I pick it up and gently shake it. It's very light for car parts. On the top is a small stamp of a cobra.

Once I make my toast, I walk upstairs with the box under my arm and set it on the bed. I check the time. 9AM. I hope this guy shows up to get the box soon, or I'll be late for my next class, and that would be really bad.

I put on my shoes and coat, so when the guy finally gets here, I can bolt out the door and drive fast to the university.

When the clock hits 10AM, I decide to call Brandon.

"Hey, babe, what are you doing?" His voice is cheery.

"Well, I'm kind of going crazy, because your guy was supposed to be here quite a while ago. I've really got to get going. Can I just leave the box on the step outside?"

"No. No way. Don't even think of doing that. Just be patient, he shouldn't be much longer."

"But I can't miss any more classes today, seriously." My anxiety is quickly rising.

"Listen, I'll give the guy a call and tell him to hurry up. Just promise me you will not leave until he gets there, no matter what."

"Fine, just please call and tell him I'm in a mad rush."

"I will. I've got to go. Hang tight. And, Sophie?"

"Yes?"

"I love you."

I hang up and take a deep breath, telling myself that everything will work out okay. The guy will show up and get the box and I will make it to class, even if I'm a few minutes late. I won't be in too much trouble as long as I show up.

I watch the clock for the next fifteen minutes, then stand up and pace the room a few times. Just as I'm about to text Brandon, I hear a loud bang coming from downstairs. It's got to be the guy.

I grab the box and sprint downstairs to the front door. As soon as I open it, I see the back of Sylvie as she makes her way to her car, starts it, and drives away.

What in the hell?

Sylvie was home the whole time I've been waiting. Why couldn't she have passed the box to the guy? It's not like she had classes to go to.

Angry, I call Brandon. Ring after ring, he doesn't answer.

Then, I send a text: *What is going on? Sylvie was home the whole time. I thought she went with you and Ryder. Couldn't she have waited for the person who's supposed to be showing up? Please call as soon as you can.*

I sit on the bottom step of the stairs and look at the time on my cell. I am now too late for my second class. Even if this guy showed up right now, I couldn't make it in time. I get up and slowly walk up the stairs to email yet another professor.

* * *

When the clock hits twelve-thirty, it's obvious that there's no way I'm going to make it to the university before every class I had today ends. Feeling depressed, I'm just about to walk back upstairs and check my computer for messages from my professors when I hear a car pull up to the front of the house.

I look out the small window and see a wiry-looking guy wearing a baseball cap getting out of a beat-up Ford. I wait until he knocks, then from behind the door I ask what he wants. When he mentions Brandon, and that he's here to pick up a box, I get the parcel with the cobra stamp from the kitchen and open the door just enough to pass the box through.

He thanks me, but I don't reply. It's because he's so late that I may get kicked out of my courses.

I watch out the window until his car leaves, then make my way upstairs. I'm just opening my emails when there's a loud rap on the downstairs door.

I can't believe this guy. First he screws up my day, and now he's forgotten something and is stealing even more time from me. I'm going to give him a piece of my mind, even if Brandon gets mad at me.

I rush down the stairs, wanting to be face to face when I unload on him. I swing the door open, then step back in shock as I stare at a man I've never seen before. He is over six feet tall, with shoulder-length, curly brown hair.

"Hi. Sorry to bother you." He smiles sheepishly. "I was just wondering if you know where the Dooleys' Vegetable Farm is? I think I'm horribly lost."

I shake my head, suddenly aware that I'm in the middle of nowhere with this stranger. "We just moved in, and I'm not familiar with the area."

"Okay. No problem." He shrugs, still smiling. "I guess I'll have to call them and get better directions."

I nod and am just about to close the door when he says, "Again, I'm sorry I disturbed you…um…what's your name?"

"It's Sophie." *Why did I tell him?*

"Nice to meet you, Sophie. I'm Darren. I'll make sure to tell the Dooleys that I met their new neighbor."

I watch him get into a shiny black muscle car and drive down the road.

As soon as I'm sure he's gone, I run upstairs and Google search The Dooley Vegetable Farm. No results show up on the page.

That's weird.

I feel creeped out. What if Darren—if that really is his name—is some sort of psychopath? What if, right now, he's plotting a way to get into the house and attack me?

I find myself wishing that Sylvie was still home. I look out the window and scan the back field. Even though I don't see him, he could be lurking around the front of the house. I gather my laptop and car keys, then move downstairs where there are more windows.

After a check of every window in the kitchen and front room, I feel a bit calmer. I want to go outside and get into my car, but I give it a few more minutes just to be absolutely certain the stranger is long gone. So, I sit on the bottom stair and open my emails.

I've gotten no responses from any of the professors I wrote. They're probably busy writing the department head about my absence. I sigh and close my laptop.

With keys in hand, I put my laptop down and get up to peer out the window. When I'm sure the coast is clear, I slowly unlock the door, then open it and poke my head out, looking at the barn and the sheds.

Stepping out on the narrow top step, I visually calculate the steps to my car. I lock the handle and pull the door shut, then turn and sprint like hell toward my car, scanning the terrain as I run.

I'm just grabbing the car door handle when I see a cloud of dust from a vehicle coming toward the house. I jump in the driver's seat and lock my door, and with shaking hands try to get the key in the ignition. Finally, the key goes in and the car starts, just as the vehicle pulls up close behind me. I look in the rear-view mirror and let out a long sigh of relief. It's Brandon.

He gets out of his truck and raps on my window. He's smiling until he sees my eyes and can tell something is wrong. I unlock the door and step out.

"Hey, beautiful, are you just getting home from classes?"

"No. I couldn't go."

"Why not?"

"If you checked your messages or answered your phone, you'd know the answer to that."

"We had no service in the hills in Chilliwack. What happened?"

"Nothing, that's just it. Your pick-up guy didn't show up until about an hour ago. I couldn't leave."

Brandon sighs. "I am so sorry, sweetie."

"Sorry or not, I don't think I'll be allowed to continue in my program now. I bet you anything I get a letter from the dean, telling me not to bother coming back." Tears start to bead in my eyes.

"It'll be okay. You'll see."

I shake my head. He's just saying that so I'll calm down. He doesn't know a thing about how a university operates.

"Why were you in your car? Were you going somewhere?"

"I just wanted to get out of the house after some guy randomly knocked on the door and freaked me out."

Brandon looks suspicious. "What guy?"

"I don't know. This guy showed up not long after your pick-up guy did. He said he was lost and was looking for some vegetable farm."

"What was he driving?"

"I don't know. A black, older muscle car."

Brandon takes his eyes off me and looks over at Ryder, who's moving boxes out of the truck. "Ryder, take the truck and drive around the area. Some guy in a black car was just here. It might be someone casing the place."

Ryder immediately sets down the box he's carrying and fires up the truck. I watch as he speeds off up the road. Brandon puts his arm around me and we walk back into the house. He tells me to go upstairs. "I'll be right up after I check the security cameras."

I flop down on the bed and cry, worried sick about the probability of being kicked out of university. It's my own fault, and I have no one to blame but myself. No matter how upsetting it was to be at my unit after

Tessa was murdered, I should've stayed there at least until the semester was finished. Now, I'm going to be aimless and floundering without my schooling.

Not to mention broke. I'm positive my mom and dad will cut me off as soon as they know I'm not attending school anymore. It will break their hearts. They worked so hard to make sure I'd have enough money to get an education and do something great with my life.

I feel so low right now. I've been selfish, only thinking about Brandon and being with him. I pull my knees up to my chest and slowly rock.

Brandon walks in and sits next to me on the bed. "Everything will work out, Soph." His voice is soft. "You'll see."

If he says that one more time, I'm going to lose it.

He gently rubs my back. "I think you need some help relaxing right now."

I watch as he goes to the bathroom cabinet and opens a large vitamin bottle, then pulls out a small baggie with blue pills inside. He then fills a glass with water and walks over to me. "Here, take this." He gives me the glass and one of the pills. "It'll make you feel a lot better."

I sit up and chase the tablet down with water, then lie back down. "Will you stay with me for a while?"

"Of course, I will." He slips in behind me.

"Was there any footage on the cameras of that guy that came to the door?"

"No. Idiot Ryder forgot to turn the cameras on."

* * *

I wake feeling extremely groggy. I look beside me, but Brandon is gone. He must be either downstairs with Ryder and Sylvie or outside working in the barn.

As soon as I sit up, I hear music and voices coming from downstairs. Feeling unsteady, I walk slowly to the washroom and splash cold water on my face. I check the time. It's just after midnight. Dizzy, and feeling a bit nauseated, I decide to go downstairs to find Brandon.

I maneuver down the steep stairs, gripping the railing as I go. When I look down, everything spins like I'm inside a tornado, so I keep my head up and feel the way with my feet. The noise from downstairs gets louder with each step I take.

Finally, I reach the bottom and, with the assistance of the walls, creep slowly toward the living room. When I get to the entrance of the small room, I see ten or fifteen people standing by the stereo and sitting on the couches.

Nobody sees me until Ryder walks past me and says, "Wow, girl. You look like you've been having a private party upstairs." He laughs and continues to the kitchen.

Trying hard to focus, I scan the crowd for my boyfriend. When I don't see him, I conclude that he must be outside in the barn, but there's no way I can make it out there until I feel less out of it.

I'm just about to begin the hard journey back upstairs when, through the noise, I hear Brandon's voice. Three or four people blocking the view of the La-Z-Boy disburse, and there, sitting behind them, is Brandon.

In his lap is a half-dressed girl. His arms are around her waist, and he's kissing her neck.

I can't believe what I'm seeing.

Why is some slut straddling my boyfriend? Why is he kissing her?

I want to scream, but I'm too dizzy. Plus, the music is so loud, nobody would hear me anyway.

Ryder returns and cruises past me, then makes his way to Brandon and points in my direction. Brandon motions for the girl to get off him. Then he stands and makes his way to where I'm leaning against the doorframe.

"Hey, beautiful," he hollers over the noise. "What are you doing down here? I thought you'd be sleeping."

I try to speak, but my voice is groggy and frail. When he goes to pull me in close, I move my arm to slap him, but I'm too weak to make contact. In one swoop, he lifts me up in his arms and carries me up the stairs.

After putting me on the bed, he sits beside me and strokes my hair. "You need to sleep, Soph."

"I'm not going to sleep. I'm leaving."

He smiles. "Oh no, you're not. You're staying here with me."

"No, I'm not. I saw you with that slut. You were making out with her."

Brandon grows quiet for a few moments, then shrugs. "Yes. That's right. I was. But that has nothing to do with us."

I shake my head, which makes the room spin even more. "I should never have fallen for you. You're a creep, and I want to go home."

He grins. "You are home, silly. You just need some more sleep. You'll see things differently in the morning."

I reach for my cell on the bedside table. He sees what I'm doing and grabs the phone before I can. "Who are you going to call?"

"Anyone. I want to get out of here. If you won't let me, then I'll call the police."

Suddenly, his self-assured expression is replaced with one of anger. He slams his hand over my mouth and pushes the back of my head deep into the pillow.

He presses his mouth to my ear. "That would be a grave mistake on your part, little girl." With his other hand, he slides my phone into his pocket. "What you're going to do is take another pill to help you relax, and then you're going back to sleep."

My heart beats fast and my hands shake. I can't believe he just shoved his hand over my mouth. I don't recognize him at all right now.

With what just happened, I'm not only too out of it to run, but now I'm scared to challenge him.

"Stay right here." He gets up and goes into the bathroom for a few moments, then returns with water and the baggie of pills. He shakes one into his hand and holds it out.

"Please, I can't take another one, I'll be a zombie. I'm still out of it from the one you gave me earlier."

His expression is hard and cold. He says nothing. He just holds the pill in front of me.

Scared, I slowly drag the tablet off his palm and put it in my mouth. I hide it under my tongue. Still silent, he hands me the water. I take a few quick sips, then lay my head back down on the pillow.

"Do you think I'm a fucking idiot?"

I shake my head.

192

He leans in close. "Open your mouth."

Again, I shake my head.

Like a striking cobra, his hand shoots out and grabs my jaw, forcing my lips to part. He crams his fingers in my mouth and roots around painfully until he locates the pill.

"Either you swallow it, or I will push it down your throat."

Tears flow down my cheeks as I swallow the pill.

"There you go, was that so hard?" He lies down next to me. "Now, I'm going to stay here for a few minutes, just to make sure you don't stick your finger down your throat."

In the silence, I close my eyes and picture my mom and dad. I talk to them in my head. *If I overdose, I love you both very much. I'm sorry I didn't listen to you about him, and now I'm paying the ultimate price.*

It doesn't take long for the first effects of the pill to hit. Before I know it, I'm struggling to stay conscious.

Chapter Ten

My stomach lurches before I can even open my eyes.

I put my hand over my mouth and quickly roll over on the bed. I swing my feet from under the covers and pull myself to a sitting position, my head spinning.

I look across the sun-filled room and focus on the bathroom, then will myself to stand on weak, shaking legs. Stumbling as I walk, I finally make it to the toilet and throw up.

My throat raw and whole body rattling, I grab the glass from beside the sink and fill it with water before gulping it down. Again, my guts churn and empty into the toilet.

With no one stopping me, I repeat the process three or four times to clean out any residual drugs in my system. Then, I lie with my cheek on the cool floor and wait until my stomach stops convulsing.

When I finally muster the energy, I make my way back to the bed and lie down. I need a few minutes to gain strength before I can figure out how the hell I'm getting out of here.

Wrapped up in the blanket beside me is Brandon, no doubt still sleeping off whatever he drank last night. I'm careful not to disturb him as I lie still with my eyes closed, waiting for the spinning to stop.

I don't hear his normal soft snoring, which means he's really out cold. Good! If he's still out when I gain the strength to get out of bed, I might have a chance to dig through his pants for my phone.

* * *

It's been about an hour since I purged my stomach, and I'm able to focus a little more. If I'm going to make a break for it, I've got to do it soon.

Just as I sit up and focus on my shoes beside the bed, I hear someone coming up the stairs. I quickly lie back down and close my eyes. The door opens, and heavy footsteps walk toward the bed, then stop.

I listen to labored breathing as whoever it is stands over Brandon and me. The only person I can imagine walking into the room is Ryder. He's here to wake up Brandon with some news about work. If that happens, I'm scared of what Brandon will do to me, knowing how aggressive and angry he was last night.

I tell myself to remain calm when he wakes up. To act all loving and agree with whatever he says. Play the part, or who knows what could happen.

"Get up." The demanding voice booms in the empty room.

But it's not Ryder's voice. It's Brandon's.

Confused, I open my eyes slightly. He's standing over me, looking just as psychotic as he did last night.

"Oh, hi." I hope he buys my agreeable demeanor.

"Get up!" he repeats.

I sit up, then look at the person lying in bed beside me. "Who's that?" I try to keep calm.

"Don't play stupid, Sophie. You know exactly who it is."

"I do?"

"Don't try to act like you don't remember. Because of what you've done, you put all of us in jeopardy."

"I don't know what you're talking about. I haven't done a thing."

He walks around the bed and grabs hold of the blanket. He keeps his furious eyes on me as he pulls the covers back.

Nothing in me was prepared to see what I did.

A young woman lies on the pillow beside me, a bluish tinge to her pale skin. Her eyes are wide open, like she's glaring at something, and there are marks on her neck. I can't breathe as I quickly shuffle off the bed and stand up, still staring at the girl.

I open my mouth to scream, but no sound comes out. Brandon covers up the body, then walks back over to my side of the bed.

"You were very jealous last night. And after you took another dose of pills that I begged you not to take, you came back downstairs and started a fight with Wendy. Everyone else left because you made such a scene. The two of you squabbled for a while, but then somehow started hitting it off. Eventually you two came up here and began making out. I didn't want to spoil your fun, so I went with Sylvie and Ryder to lock up the barn.

"When I finally came back upstairs, you were choking Wendy and she had lost consciousness. I called for Sylvie and Ryder to help, and we tried everything we could to revive her, but it was too late. They'll testify to that. You passed out right after."

I stare at him in disbelief. I know he doesn't believe what he just said. I can tell by his shifting eyes. And even though I haven't been in a relationship with him for very long, he can tell I know the whole story he just spewed is bullshit.

I look back at Wendy, and tears roll down my cheeks. She was someone's child, and no doubt has a family that will be looking for her. I think about Tessa, and how deeply her death affected the ones that loved her.

"It's a little late for crying."

I look back at him. "You can't actually believe I'm capable of killing someone."

He shrugs. "I was surprised, that's for sure. As were Ryder and Sylvie. But I guess when you down pills all night, you can turn into a monster."

I'm not the monster here, you son-of-a-bitch. You did this, or Ryder did. But not me. I was so drugged out I could barely move, too weak to walk properly because of what you forced down my throat. Try all you like to sell me this story, but in my heart of hearts, I know who's responsible.

I'm about to suggest calling the cops until I remember how crazy he got when I mentioned calling them last night. So I say nothing.

Brandon tells me to go and have a shower because I look like a slob. Then he calls Ryder upstairs. When I'm in the bathroom, I put my ear firmly to the door and listen. After a moment, I hear Ryder enter the bedroom. Brandon tells him they have to get rid of the body. When Ryder asks where they're going, Brandon replies, "Cultus Lake."

They're throwing that poor girl's body into that frigid lake? I try to think how I can prevent that from happening, but I'm in real danger of ending up like her. I'm just glad she won't be aware of what they're about to do with her body, the blatant disregard by treating her like a piece of trash.

Worried that Brandon will catch me listening in, I turn on the shower and step in. The warm water rushes over my skin. I lather as much soap on me as I can, but no matter how hard I scrub, I still feel dirty.

By the end of the shower, my head feels clearer. I start thinking of ways to get away from here. Then I remember what Brandon told me, about he, Sylvie, and Ryder all witnessing the crime I'd apparently committed. I've watched enough cop shows to know how common it is for innocent people to get convicted because of false witnesses. I'm sure I'd be exonerated if Wendy's body is found, but if it isn't, I could be in jail for a very long time.

Getting kicked out of school would break my parents' hearts. My being in jail for murder would kill them.

Just the thought of their pain makes tears roll down my face. I don't see any way out of this that won't tear them apart, except to bide my time and do what Brandon says until I think of a proper plan.

When I come out of the shower, Wendy's body is wrapped in a sheet and Ryder has her flung over his shoulder like a rag doll. The sight makes me nauseated, and I fight to keep from throwing up again.

Brandon looks out of breath as he strips the bed. He glances up at me. "Do you see the mess you're putting us through?"

Nice try! I feel like saying. Instead, I put my head down and walk to the dresser for clothes. I can feel his eyes on me as I pull out a pair of tights and a sweatshirt.

"You know, it kind of turned me on that you were so jealous last night."

Is he serious?

I feel like I've been thrust into the twilight zone. A young girl is dead, and he's thinking about being turned on? How the hell did he keep this psychotic part of his character from me while we were together? It's like he's void of compassion and decency.

It's the part of him my mom could see. If I make it out of this hell in one piece, I'll never doubt her again.

Thankfully, Ryder comes back up the stairs and diverts Brandon's focus from me. "Are you ready to go, boss?"

"Get Sylvie up here first." Brandon grabs my car keys and puts them in his pocket.

Ryder goes to the top of the stairs and whistles, like he's calling a dog. A few moments later, Sylvie is standing in the doorway.

Brandon tells her that he and Ryder will be leaving for a while, and he needs her to keep an eye on me.

"I'm no babysitter," she scoffs.

Ryder walks over to her and lifts his hand in warning. She immediately winces, and both men laugh.

I was right about Ryder all along. He does hit Sylvie. The only difference now is that no one is faking who they are anymore.

When the men finally leave, I stay in my room and look out the window, thinking about how to get out of my predicament. I have no ally in this mess, no phone, and no laptop to…wait a minute.

My laptop. Where did I put it?

Then, I remember. I left it near the stairwell when I ran to my car yesterday.

I tip-toe to the bedroom door and slowly open it, then peer down the stairwell. There's a small flicker of hope when I don't see or hear Sylvie.

I quietly ease onto the first step. So far, the coast is clear, and I cautiously creep down a few more steps. I'm halfway down now, my eyes scanning the bottom floor for my laptop, and for any sign of Sylvie.

Step by step, I make my way down the staircase until I'm almost at the bottom. My eyes flick to the front door, and for a second I picture myself opening it and running as fast as I can up the dirt road. The vision doesn't last long when I remember

Brandon's claim of them being eyewitnesses to my crime. If I did run, it would take too long for me to reach the police before Brandon disposes of the body and calls the police first. Not only would I have him chasing me down, but I'd have the whole police department on my tail as well.

The best thing I can do is get to my computer and email my mother about what's happened. Maybe if she calls the cops and shows them my email, it will help them believe my innocence and they can catch Brandon with his guard down.

When I reach the bottom, my eyes search every surface for my laptop. Sylvie must be in her room, as I can't hear any noise coming from the living room or the kitchen. Maybe if I glide my feet smoothly across the floor, I can make it to the other rooms without being heard.

As soon as I take the first step, I hear a thump from a room down the hall.

I look behind me at the tall staircase, knowing there's no way I'm making it back to my room without Sylvie catching me. As the footsteps grow closer, I dart into the hall closet. There's no door, but thankfully there are numerous winter jackets I can conceal myself with.

I can feel the vibrations of her footsteps on the old wooden floor as she nears. My heart is pounding so hard, I feel like it could burst from my chest. My legs are shaking so badly, I can almost hear them rattle.

The footsteps stop at the bottom of the stairwell. I'm only a few feet from her. Closing my eyes tightly, I pray that the next sound I hear is her turning around and walking back down the hall, but everything is silent.

In one fell swoop, Sylvie pushes the coats to one side. Terrified, I stare at her stark, cold face as she glares at me.

"Sylvie, I was just coming downstairs to get something to eat, and I—"

"Save the bullshit, Sophie."

"Okay. I will. I'm sorry." I begin to cry.

"Get the fuck out of the closet."

I watch her hands as I step in front of her.

She looks me up and down. "Well, at least you made it through the night." Her voice is low.

"What do you mean?"

"You saw what happened to that other girl. You're lucky it wasn't you."

My jaw drops. "You know I didn't kill her? Brandon said you and Ryder saw me strangle that girl, and you would both testify against me."

Sylvie looks up at the camera at the entrance, then grabs me by the arm and pulls me down the hall to the kitchen. She lets go in front of the table and gestures for me to sit on one of the chairs. "Keep your voice down. Do you hear me?"

I nod, grateful that she hasn't beaten the crap out of me already.

"If you want to make it out alive, you'll have to play the game."

"What game?"

"Wake up, little girl. Use your brain."

"I'm sorry. I'm not trying to make you mad, I just don't understand what you mean by playing the game."

Sylvie shakes her head. "You should've listened to me on the Island. You should've left then. Now, it's too late. Not only are you in danger, but you're also fucking up all my plans, too."

I gulp back tears. "I didn't mean to. I'm so sorry."

"Play things smart. Don't ask questions. Don't create waves. Do exactly as you're told and maybe you'll get out of this."

"I don't understand. If you don't want to be here, why can't we just leave right now? Ryder and Brandon are busy throwing that poor girl's body into the lake. We could probably make it to the police before they get back. Do you have a car?"

Sylvie reaches into her pocket and pulls out a set of car keys. I jump out of the chair, crying with relief. "That's great. Let's go."

"Sit back down."

"I don't understand. Why won't you leave?"

"Because, Sophie, there's more than me to think about here."

"Ryder? Are you saying you don't want to leave because you care about Ryder? He beats you—why are you loyal to him?"

She reaches out and grabs onto my shoulder hard. "If you say a word about what I tell you, I swear I will do nothing to help you, and your fate will be sealed. Do you understand me?"

I nod.

"Ryder and I had a child five years ago. Her name is Faith. We got really messed up on dope, and she was taken from us and placed in the care of Ryder's nasty mother. I sobered up right away, even though Ryder didn't. He's got his mother under his thumb, and she won't let me see my little girl without Ryder being there. In the meantime, I have to do whatever he tells me so I can visit my little girl."

A tear rolls down her cheek. This is the first time I've seen her show any emotion besides disdain and anger. Now, I know why. "That's terrible, Sylvie. I am so sorry."

"It's just the way it is. Until you came along, I'd been trying to get proof of Ryder and Brandon's dealings so I have a chance at getting my daughter back."

"What do you mean, dealings?"

"You can't be this naïve. You must've suspected something was off when you had to give that guy a parcel and you couldn't just leave it on the steps."

"I don't know. I was so preoccupied with missing classes that I don't think past that."

Sylvie shakes her head in disappointment. "You are definitely innocent."

"I'm sorry. I'm trying to understand. Are you suggesting there was something else besides car stuff in the box? Like drugs or something?"

"Bingo. Give the girl a prize."

"There were drugs in that box? Really? Brandon sells drugs?"

She nods.

"Is that what he did while you and Ryder were living with him above the autobody shop?"

"What autobody shop?"

I stare at her in disbelief. "Are you serious? He told me that the three of you were living together in a small apartment above his work."

She scoffs. "Brandon hasn't had an honest job in his life, except maybe while he was doing time. And neither one of those fools could fix a car if their lives depended on it."

Finally, she sits down at the table next to me and fills me in on everything I thought I knew about Brandon. How everything he told me was a lie. He never took the rap for his thieving cousin. He was a drug dealer, and got busted in a meth lab in Surrey. As for his parents, that was all a big lie, too. His mother and father both died of alcoholism a few years back.

I put my head in my hands. "But why did he pick me to be with? I'm so far away from that world. It must've been hard for him to act like another person the whole time we were together."

"He likes young girls who don't have a lot of friends and family around. He gets off on preying on girls like you."

"I want him to get what's coming to him."

"I do, too. Ryder, as well. But until then, we have to be super cautious. You're a sweet girl, Sophie. But if anything you do jeopardizes my chance of getting my daughter back, I won't even think twice about throwing you under the bus."

I nod. "What can I do? How can I help you get what you need on Ryder and Brandon?"

"Nothing. Just be obedient to Brandon, play the part, and stay the hell out of my way. I know this game, you don't."

I nod. "Okay. But you'll help me?"

"I'll help us. Yes."

"And after you get what you need on Ryder and Brandon, you'll tell the cops that I never touched Wendy?"

"I promise, if I gather enough proof to help me get my child back, I will testify that you weren't the one to kill that girl. I actually saw some of what happened last night after Brandon brought you upstairs. He came down a while later and kicked everyone out. Everyone but Wendy."

"What happened next?"

"Ryder, Brandon, and she sat in the living room, doing coke for hours. I was in my room. Then Ryder told me to make him some food, so I came out to the kitchen. I heard Wendy getting mouthy with Brandon—she sounded really high. Brandon told her to shut her mouth, and she called him a pussy. He slapped her and she slapped him back. Then Ryder came into the kitchen and said to go back to the room. I didn't see or hear anything after that."

"So he killed her, then put her in bed? Why would he do that?"

"How should I know what's in his crazy head? Maybe he thought you were going to leave and needed a way to keep you here."

Just then, her cell beeps. It's a message from Ryder. Sylvie tells me to go back upstairs, as the men will be home soon.

I'm just heading out of the kitchen when a question pops into my head. I turn back. "Sylvie. Thank you for trusting me enough to talk to me. As scared as I am, I don't feel as alone in this now. Is it okay if I ask you one more question?"

"What?"

"My roommate Tessa was found murdered at Cultus Lake. She'd been strangled, like Wendy. You don't know if Brandon had anything to do with that, do you?"

"That's enough talking for one day. Go back upstairs now, and wait for Brandon."

I put my head down and walk up the hallway. When I get to the bottom of the stairs, she hurries up behind me. "Wait, Sophie. If you're given a pill, stash it between your upper teeth and gums. For some reason, they don't check there."

I nod, feeling relieved. "Thank you."

When I get upstairs, I make the bed and think about poor Wendy, and how devastated her family will be. Brandon is the devil. And I'm stuck here with him.

Until Sylvie and I can leave, I'll have to do whatever I can to convince him I'm a team player.

I sit and stare out the window, thinking about everything Sylvie told me. I'm so relieved she trusted me when she doesn't even know me. And I can't believe she's been stuck with a man she loathes for so long. She must be an incredibly strong person.

I look out at the barn, where Brandon and Ryder have been spending so much of their time. I wish I'd have thought to ask Sylvie what really goes on in there. Now I'm wondering what the meetings were really about on the Island. I could've been in the truck with Brandon while he was transporting drugs.

The thought makes my stomach queasy. No wonder Brandon was so ignorant to the ferry worker when he tried to help secure the tarp on the truck.

* * *

The front door opens and closes, and I hear the two men's voices. Not knowing what to do, I grab a cloth from under the bathroom sink and start wiping the surfaces. Footsteps approach, and the bedroom door opens. My body shivers and a heavy weight presses on my chest.

"Hey, beautiful. Come and sit with me for a minute on the bed. I want to talk to you."

His voice is warm and sweet, like it was the whole time he was deceiving me. I put down the cloth and go sit beside him on the bed, hoping he doesn't pick up on how frantic I'm feeling.

He reaches out to put his hand on my leg, and I jump.

"Whoa. Look at you, all nervous of me. Didn't you say you love me?"

"I do love you," I lie. "One bad night isn't going to change that."

"Really? Because the whole time I was gone, I was a little worried that you meant what you said this morning, about wanting to leave me."

"I was just jealous about Wendy, and the attention you were giving her. But now she got what she deserved, so I have you all to myself again." I force a smile.

He raises an eyebrow, looking skeptical. "Is that right?"

"Of course it is. I'm sorry for what I said. I've got to learn not to be such a grudge-holder."

"Those are great words, Sophie. But I'm going to need you to prove what you're saying. Can you do that?"

"I would do anything to prove how I feel."

"Well, that's good. If you'll do anything, I want you to make a call for me."

"A call? To whom?"

He smiles. "To your parents."

"My parents? But why?" I put my hand on his. "They have nothing to do with us."

His eyebrows furrow and he looks at me with sharp eyes. "I knew it. You're bullshitting me because you're afraid."

"Brandon. Don't be silly. You're all that matters to me. I just don't understand why you want me to call my mom and dad." I shake my head. "But you know what? It doesn't really matter. Give me the phone, and I'll call right now. Just tell me what you want me to say."

He stares at me for a few more moments, then seems to relax. He pulls my cell phone from his pocket. "I want you to tell them that we're getting married."

He can't be serious. That will destroy my parents. They're already worried about me. He stares into my eyes as I do my best not to project my anxiety.

"Okay. Sure. Just hand me the phone, and I'll do it."

"Put it on speaker so I can hear everything."

"Okay. Whatever you want," I say, as my heart is breaking.

He passes me the phone and I scroll through my contacts until I find my parents' number. I take a deep breath, then look at Brandon and grin.

The phone rings three times. I'm about to tell him that they're probably sleeping, and that we'll have to try them later, my mother's tired voice answers the phone.

Why Mom? Why didn't you just let the call go to the answering machine?

"Hi, Mom. It's me."

"Sophie. What's wrong? Why are you calling at this hour?"

Brandon elbows me hard, causing me to wince. "I have some news that couldn't wait, and I needed to tell you right away."

"That jerk Brandon hasn't done anything to you, has he?"

"Watch what you say, Mom," Brandon hollers. "I'm sitting right here."

There are a few moments of silence. Then my mom says, "Sophie. What is this about?" She sounds flustered and worried.

"I...I just want you to be the first one to know that...that Brandon asked me to marry him. And I said yes."

I'm sorry Mom. I had no choice. I love you so much, and I promise I'll tell you everything that's happened as soon as I get away from here. Please don't worry about me.

"Sophie? Have you completely taken leave of your senses?"

"I don't know what you mean." I force confidence while I'm trying not to cry.

"I don't know what this is about, Brandon, but there's no way you are marrying my child. You can get that thought straight out of your head."

Brandon laughs. "Aw, come on, Mom. Is that any way to speak to your soon-to-be son-in-law?"

"Sophie. Call me when you're alone. We need to talk!"

My mind is whirling frantically. "We're busy getting settled in our new place, so it may be a while."

"I don't give a damn. Get a hold of me soon. And until you do, you better not marry him."

I take a breath. "The bottom line is that I love Brandon. I love him even more than I loved Mr. Swansson."

Brandon jerks, then speaks into the phone, "By Mom," before hanging up. He glares at me. "Who is Mr. Swansson? Are you trying to pull a fast one?"

I force a laugh. "No. Of course not. Mr. Swansson was a teddy bear I won as a child in a jellybean-guessing contest at our neighborhood store. The name of the shop was called Swansson's Grocery. I took that bear everywhere with me. I had him right up to when I started living in residence on campus." I can hardly believe the story I'd just adlibbed.

He stares at me, deciding if he'll accept what I've just said. As calmly as I can, I look back at him.

"Okay," he finally says. "I believe you."

"Well, you should. It's true."

Brandon takes my phone and puts it back into his pocket, then gets up and walks to the door. "Get dressed. We're going out for a while."

I wait until I hear him walk down the stairs before I let the tears flow.

Please, Mom. Please remember that Mr. Swansson was the police officer that brought me home when I was little after I fell off my bike. My parents were so grateful that my mother invited him and his family over for a Bar-B-Q.

I get up and walk to the bathroom to splash cold water on my face. If Brandon detects that I've been crying, he'll know I'm lying to him. I dress as fast as I can, then put cover-up under my eyes and brush my hair. Just as I'm putting on my trainers, Brandon yells from downstairs: "Sophie, get your ass down here."

When we walk outside, Sylvie and Ryder are already in their car. Brandon and I get into the backseat. Brandon tells Ryder to head for the Chinese restaurant downtown. I guess murdering Wendy and disposing of her body in the lake really worked up his appetite.

If something happens to me before Sylvie can get us out of this horrible situation, I hope Brandon pays gravely for what he's done.

As we come to the end of the gravel road, Ryder asks Brandon about getting security alarms in the house. Just as we turn onto the paved road, I glance at the abandoned motel on the corner and notice the front end of a black muscle car peeking out from behind the building.

No one else seems to notice, and I say nothing. I hope, if it is that Darren guy and he was casing out the farmhouse, that he breaks in while we're gone and steals every bit of drugs in the place.

The four of us sit at a corner table in the restaurant. Even though the last thing on my mind is eating, I order a combo dish so Brandon doesn't get suspicious. I need him to think that nothing is bothering me. Ryder and Brandon are engrossed in conversation when I tell Brandon I have to use the bathroom. As soon as I stand, Ryder tells Sylvie to go with me.

Once inside the restroom, Sylvie tells me to keep playing it cool in front of Brandon and, more importantly, not to let on that she and I are talking. "They need to believe that we don't like each other, otherwise they'll get paranoid and we won't be left alone together."

I agree, and after we're finished in the washroom, we hurry back to the table. The waitress is leaning over the table, flirting with Brandon. When she turns and sees me, she straightens up and asks if there's anything else she can get us.

Brandon smiles at her. "I can think of a few things."

What a pig. I think back to weeks ago, how he'd somehow gotten into my residential building for an impromptu visit. I'd assumed he'd slipped unseen past someone leaving the building. Now, though, I realize how easy he would've found it to convince a student to open the door. That's what he's good at—charming innocent girls who think he's gorgeous. But to me, after what he's done, I find him hideous.

When she walks away, Brandon watches like a horny dog until she's out of sight. Then he turns his attention to the rest of us. "From now on, we'll have to work fast and put in long hours. The demand is high right now. If we work hard, there's a shitload of money to be made."

Ryder looks at Sylvie. "You have to pack boxes a lot faster than you've been doing. You work like a fucking turtle."

Brandon laughs, then gets a serious look on his face as he turns to me. "Your job is to pass boxes to people that come to the door. It'll be the same guys picking up every time, so it's foolproof. They'll all have envelopes that you give to Sylvie. Got it?"

"Yes, of course."

As we leave the restaurant, Brandon looks up at the neon sign above the tattoo shop a few stores down. He grins. "Come on, you guys. I've got a great idea."

Once we're inside, Sylvie and I sit on a red torn couch as Ryder and Brandon talk to the heavily tattooed bald man behind the counter. After a few moments, Brandon waves me over.

I hope to hell he's not thinking I'm going to get a tattoo. At least not one that he chooses.

"Happy birthday," the bald guy says. "Your old man here tells me you want to get his name inked onto your hip. Is that right?"

Brandon steps hard on my foot. I wince in pain, then smile. "Okay."

The tattoo artist leans over the counter and looks in my eyes. "Be sure, sweetie. I always warn young people about getting a name tattooed on them because sometimes, most times, relationships end ugly. Then you're stuck with the person's name on you forever."

Brandon glances at me. "We have an unbreakable bond. We're lifers."

I nod as the horror of what's about to happen hits me. I love artwork on people. There are some beautiful tats out there. But the thought of getting this murderous pig's name inked into my flesh like a brand makes me sick.

Brandon and I are led into a back room, and I'm asked to hop up onto what looks like a dentist's chair. The tattooist asks me to undo and lower my jeans, and tell him where I want the tattoo. Brandon points to my left side and smiles.

The bald man gets his equipment ready. Just as he's about to start, he looks at me intently and repeats the question. "Are you sure?"

Of course I'm not sure. You're about to brand me for life with the name of a devil.

As Brandon leers at me, I nod in agreement.

I hear the whirring of the tattoo gun, and I close my eyes. As the needle punctures my skin and injects the ink, all I think about is ways I can get rid of it after I escape from Brandon. I don't care if I have to burn it off. I'd rather have a hideous scar than his name on me.

It doesn't take long before the machine stops and the man is getting a bandage ready.

"It looks great," Brandon says. "Look at it, Sophie."

I don't want to. I would rather pretend it's not there.

Brandon nudges me, and I'm forced to look. If it was another Brandon, and on someone else's hip, it would be a nice tattoo. The guy definitely has skill. But knowing whom this tattoo represents, it's the ugliest thing I've ever seen.

After Brandon pays the man, the four of us walk out of the shop and get into the car. This time, Sylvie is sitting in the backseat with me. While men talk in the front, Sylvie quickly touches my leg. I know it's her way of trying to make me feel better, but I don't. I feel dirty and forever marked with the name of a monster I have come to fear and loathe.

When we're just about to turn on the gravel road, I look at the old motel and notice that the black muscle car is gone.

Back at the house, Brandon tells me to go upstairs and put something sexy on. He says that he has to work for a while in the barn with Ryder, but he'll be up soon. I cringe at the thought of his touch and, for a moment, wish that I was drunk or knocked out so I wouldn't have to be aware of whatever he wants to do to me.

I cry because it's safe to. And after I lie in bed, wearing my short slip nightie, I close my eyes and try to imagine a peaceful place with aqua-blue waters, warm white sand, and a gentle breeze washing over me. It's only when I hear footsteps on the stairs that I am yanked out of my safe picture and back into my living nightmare.

"Hey, beautiful. Wake up. I'm here."

My muscles tighten and my pulse speeds up. I open my eyes to Brandon looking down at me.

"You never thanked me for getting you the tattoo." He grins. "Here's your chance."

I don't know how I'm going to get through this. The only chance I have to convince him that I'm into it is pretending I'm with someone else—a good person who cares about me, and wouldn't do anything to cause me harm.

Chapter Eleven

One day melds into the next. I become a robot. A slave to Brandon.

I fulfill my duty and pass the sealed boxes to clients, then take their envelopes of money and give them to Sylvie. Brandon and Ryder spend the majority of daylight hours in the barn, creating more product, and Sylvie packages everything up into sealed little boxes. When I get stressed thinking about all of the drugs I'm forced to sell going into the community and killing people, Brandon often senses my demeanor and orders me to take a pill. I don't even bother to hide it in my mouth. I swallow it, which helps numb the pain of my current reality.

Last night, there was a party downstairs. Sylvie told me about the waitress that came over, and how Brandon and she had sex on the kitchen table. *Good!* I thought. The more sex he gets from other girls, the less I have to put out.

Because of the cameras in the house, and the chance of either Ryder or Brandon suddenly walking in, Sylvie and I have barely spoken over the past week. I just hope she's closer to gathering what she needs on Ryder so we can get out of this hell.

Sometimes, my mind drifts to my parents. No police came, so my message about Mr. Swansson didn't work, and my mother took my phone call at face-value. My heart breaks when I think about the damage I've done to them, a guilt that the pills help ease.

Last night I had a beautiful dream where I stood beside Cultus Lake, where Tess was found, and where Wendy still is. I wore a flowy dress and there was a warm, welcoming wind embracing me. I stepped slowly into the still water, the soft sand squishing between my toes. The farther I ventured into the lake, the more my fear, pain, and guilt went away, until the water was over my head and all that was left to feel was good.

Some moments, when things are too real, I think I could do it. I could end my life to make my hell stop. At least I wouldn't have to worry about Brandon taking me out. And I'd much rather die by my own hand than in the clutches of that beast.

* * *

The last of the sun dips between the mountains and gives way to the clear, cold night. Just as I hand off the last of the boxes on my list, Ryder swings the front door open and yells for Sylvie. As she comes out of the bedroom and passes me in the kitchen, I notice another black eye.

"You and Sophie need to pick these things up at the drugstore." He passes her a list, then gestures to me. "Brandon said to not let her out of your sight."

Sylvie nods, then looks at me coldly and tells me to go get ready.

My heart lifts as I head upstairs. Finally, we get to leave the house together. Even though we have to come back, I'll be able to talk openly to her. There's so much I need to ask her, especially about Tessa's death, about Wendy, and whether the body has been found.

I get ready as quickly as I can, then wait for Sylvie at the bottom of the stairs. When she comes down the hall, I notice she's wearing a lot of makeup to hide her bruised eye. She points to the door, and I'm just about to open it when Brandon comes in.

He looks at Sylvie. "If she pulls any shit while you guys are out, Sylvie, call me and I'll come get her." Then, he redirects his gaze to me. "Here's your chance to prove to me that you're loyal. If you fuck it up, you'll never get another chance."

I nod obediently, a shiver running over my skin.

He goes into his wallet and pulls out a wad of cash, which he hands to Sylvie. "After you pick up the items on the list, go to the drive-thru and get us some food."

He points at me like an angry parent, then turns and walks outside. I take a deep breath and Sylvie and I walk outside to the car.

Once we're on the gravel road and the farmhouse is fading in the rear-view mirror, I put my face in my hands and sob. "I can't do it, Sylvie. I can't take it anymore. I feel like a shaken bottle every second of every day. There's so much pressure and I can't take it."

With one hand on the wheel, she reaches out with the other and pats me on the back. "Stop this, Sophie. Pull it together. Our lives depend on both of us keeping a clear head. Otherwise, we don't have a chance."

When the gravel road ends and we veer onto the pavement, I glance out the passenger side window at the motel. As we pass by, I turn my head to look around the back. Sure enough, I see the black car.

"What are you looking at?" Sylvie says.

"Nothing. I thought I saw an animal."

"Our lives are at risk, and you're worried about some stupid animal?" she scoffs. "That's rich."

"Please drive slowly, Sylvie. I want to be away from the house as long as possible."

"So do I, but if either of those heathens is paying attention to the time, I'll get an angry phone call and we'll both be in trouble when we get back."

As soon as we hit the on-ramp to Highway 1, I feel a small flicker of myself returning. The road that leads to the university isn't far from here. My mind flashes back to living in my unit with Tessa. As much as I would get frustrated by all of her distractions, the memory is paradise, now.

Tessa...I can ask Sylvie anything right now.

"Tell me about Tessa, please. I need to know. Did you hear anything at all about her?

"Why do you ask?"

"Because there are similarities between how she died and the way Wendy died. Both girls were strangled. I'm not sure if Wendy had pills in her stomach, but they found pills in Tessa's stomach that contained Fentanyl."

"Let's say I do know something about your friend. What will you do with the information?"

"Absolutely nothing, I promise. At least, not until we get away from Brandon and Ryder for good."

Sylvie sighs. "Okay. Yes."

Confused, I stare at her. "Yes, what? Yes, you knew Tessa?"

"I never knew her, but I saw her. We were delivering pills to some young guys that live near the university, and your friend was talking to these guys when Brandon passed over the pills. Tessa and he recognized each other."

I shake my head. "Oh no."

Sylvie glances at me. "Are you sure you want to hear this?"

"No. But I have to know what happened."

"All right. Well, I think Brandon got a little paranoid, thinking she'd tell you that she saw him dealing. So he offered her a ride home. We only lived a few minutes away, so Brandon drove Ryder and me back to the shack we were living in, then the two of them drove off. It wasn't until an hour later that Brandon called Ryder and said he needed help with something. They were out for two or three hours, and their clothes were wet and muddy when they got back. It struck me as weird at the time, and knowing what those two are capable of, I was worried about what happened to the girl."

Tears sting my cheeks. "He consoled me when Tessa went missing, and all the while he was the one responsible for her disappearance. And, when the medical examiner found Fentanyl in her system, Brandon judged Tessa for indulging in such a dangerous drug. What a heartless bastard."

"I'm sorry, Sophie. She was very young."

"No younger than that Wendy girl." I sniff back tears. "After they came home, did you hear anything else about Tessa?'"

"Not really. Just the odd question Brandon would ask Ryder in front of me, like if Ryder remembered the pill baggy and her phone."

"Her phone?" I gasp. "Sylvie, after Tessa disappeared, I got a call from her number. When I answered, no one was there. I tried to call her back, but it went straight to voicemail."

She nods. "After Tessa's disappearance hit the news, I started thinking that her phone would sure be a good thing to implicate Brandon and Ryder in her murder."

"Yes. It sure would be." I sigh with frustration. "Brandon and Ryder have probably long disposed of it by now."

"I'm sure that was their intention." There's a half-smile on her face. "They threw it in a box to dispose of later, but when we moved, the box somehow went missing. Isn't that a bitch?"

I gape at her. "Sylvie. You have Tessa's phone? Are you serious?"

She grins fully. "All part of my master plan."

When we reach the small pharmacy in the roughest part of town, Sylvie doesn't make me come in with her. Instead, I sit and look out the window at all the people walking around, free, and seemingly carefree. If I'm lucky enough to get out of the hell I'm in, and I get the chance to be a normal person again, I will never take my life for granted again. Most importantly, I'll find a way back into my parents' lives. I know if I could just explain everything to them, they'd understand. At least, I hope they will.

Sylvie walks out of the drugstore with a paper bag in her hand and gets behind the wheel. "Ryder called twice while I was in the pharmacy. He wants us back there right after we go through the drive-thru."

I don't know how I'm going to gather enough strength to be under Brandon's control anymore. I've been through as much as I can handle. "I'm scared I won't be able to take anymore, Sylvie."

"We talked about this. We're nearing the finish line. You just have to hold on for a little while longer. Do you want to be blamed for a murder you didn't commit? And even if you weren't convicted, could you sleep knowing Brandon is out there somewhere? He'll never let you go. He hates to lose. You'd be a sitting duck wherever you run to. He knows so many people in this town."

"How long?"

"I don't know. I'm working on something—"

"No! Either you tell me what you have left to gather on Ryder and Brandon, or I swear I'm going to jump out at the next red light." I slam my fists on the dashboard.

"Fine, just calm down! I'll probably need your help, anyway."

"Keep talking."

"Since we moved into the farmhouse, I've been waiting for Brandon and Ryder to set up their little pill lab in the barn so I can take pictures of everything and show them to the cops. But, I have two big hurdles to conquer first."

"What are they?"

"I can't get past the cameras inside and outside the property. Even if I waited for the guys to leave, they'd see me snooping around."

"And the other hurdle?"

"There's a steel faceplate and a lock on the barn door, and only Brandon and Ryder have a key to open it."

As we pull up at the burger joint drive-thru, I try to think of ways to help Sylvie get into the barn, but nothing comes to mind. She drives fast on the way home; I can see in her face how scared she is of Ryder and what he'll do if she doesn't do exactly what he orders.

By the time the old motel comes into view, my stomach is in knots and there's a hard lump forming in my throat. I look at the motel as we pass. The windows are mostly all knocked out, and the once-lit neon sign looks like it could fall down with a strong enough wind.

"Wait!" I holler. "That's it."

Sylvie jumps and the car swerves. "What?"

"The dark sign on the motel!"

"What are you talking about?"

"Can't we wait until Brandon and Ryder go somewhere, and then cut the power? The cameras would shut off, wouldn't they?"

Sylvie pulls the car over and looks at me. "Yes. That could work. Ryder hard wired them into the house, so if there's no power inside, the cameras won't work." She grins. "I can't believe I never thought of that. I kept wondering how to cover them up."

"As for the whole key issue, I'm not sure what to do about that yet."

"I know, me either." She reaches out and touches my hand. "You're all right, kid. You've got a good head on your shoulders. We've just got to stay in the game until we think of something."

I can feel the thick, negative energy as we pull up to the house. Sylvie turns off the car and just as we're getting out with the food and supplies, the barn door swings open and Ryder rages toward us.

Sylvie shuts the car door and braces herself. When he's arm length away, he swings a fist and makes contact with Sylvie's jaw. She staggers and screams in pain. "What? What's wrong? What did I do?"

He doesn't answer. He just winds up and punches her again. This time, she falls to the ground. In between her grunts of pain, she begs him to stop. Without thinking, I run around the car and holler. "Leave her alone. She's had enough."

There's a powerful tug on the back of my hair. Brandon pulls my head backward and presses his mouth hard to my ear. "Stay the fuck out of it. Get upstairs and wait for me."

On my way up the steps, I hear Brandon say to Ryder, "Make sure she doesn't bleed on our food."

I pace the floor of the small room, praying that Brandon isn't going to hurt me as badly as Ryder is hurting Sylvie. My heart pounds and my hands shake and I try to think of what to say to Brandon when he gets up here.

Then, when I hear the first footsteps on the stairs, my ability to think goes out the window and my head spins. Terrified, I stand by the bed, look down, and wait.

When the door bursts open, my chest tightens, and whatever air I had in my lungs escapes. I don't want to look at him, but I can't help it. If he's going to hit me like Ryder decked Sylvie, I want to see it coming so I can brace myself.

He charges across the room at me, and when he gets close, I see his expression—a sinister look of power.

His hand moves quickly. I put my arms up to stop the blow, but instead of connecting with me, his hand swings around to the back of his jeans. When he brings his hand back in view, there's a gun in it.

My knees instantly weaken and I have to fight to keep standing. He lunges forward and pushes the small barrel into my temple. "That was very sweet of you to try and protect your friend. Since you two are such close buddies now, it's going to be hard to trust either one of you anymore. You two hens may try and hatch a plan." He presses the gun harder against my head. "So, what am I going to do about that?"

"She isn't my friend, Brandon. I hate her. I only tried to make Ryder stop because I hate violence. But I shouldn't have done that, and I'm very sorry. I promise, I'll never—"

"I don't believe a fucking word coming out of your mouth."

"Please, Brandon. Don't hurt me. I love you. And as for that witch, I couldn't care less what happens between Ryder and her. That's their business."

"Stay in this room until I get back. I'll decide what to do with you when I finish in the barn."

My eyes follow him as he lets go and, like a trail of darkness, walks out with a slam of the door.

I fight to suck in small puffs of air as I sprint to the door and press my ear hard against it. I quietly sob as I hear Ryder talk to Brandon at the bottom of the stairs. "Maybe next time, that stupid bitch won't dawdle in town." He laughs.

"Come on, man," Brandon says. "We've got to finish the batch in the barn."

The front door closes and I quietly tiptoe down the stairwell. When I get to the bottom, I look out the window and see the back of Ryder going through the barn door before it closes.

I rush down the hallway and through the kitchen just as Sylvie's bedroom door creaks open. As soon as I see her face, my first thought is that she needs to get to a hospital. Her swelling lips are split in numerous places and bleeding profusely down her chin, dripping onto her clothes. However, what's concerning me most is the large, protruding bump just above her eyebrow.

I grab her elbow and help her into the kitchen. Once she's seated at the table, I grab a big handful of paper towel and wet it, then hand it to her. "Why did he do this to you?" I whisper.

"Because he can," she manages to say, wiping at the blood on her face.

"We have to get out of here, Sylvie. We won't make it. Ryder is a psycho and Brandon has a gun."

Her eyes meet mine. "A gun?"

I nod. "No matter what, we can't stay here any longer."

She's trying to grin, but can't because of the cuts. "It's okay. I have an idea of how to get into the barn now."

I feel a tiny spark of hope. "You do? How?"

"They're leaving this afternoon to do a big delivery in Chilliwack. I'll show you then."

Then, a loud noise booms though the kitchen, making both of us jump. Someone just swung the front door open so hard it crashed into the wall.

I back away from Sylvie just as Brandon trudges into the kitchen.

He sees me and Sylvie and stops. "What do we have here?" His eyes land on me. "I thought I fucking told you to stay upstairs."

"I was thirsty, so I came down."

Then, in a stroke of genius, Sylvie fights past the pain and jumps off the chair, gesturing to me harshly. "Why is this bitch in my face? I have to put up with enough shit, I don't need this babbling no-mind in my way. I'll tell you, like I told her—if she's in my way again, I'll kick the living shit out of her."

I snort back at her. "Fuck you. This kitchen isn't just for you and Ryder. It belongs to all of us."

Brandon doesn't say anything for a few scary moments, then barks, "Sophie, get your ass back upstairs and leave Sylvie alone. I've got enough going on. I don't need to hear you two squabbling."

As I make my way up the staircase, I smile. *Good job, Sylvie. Brandon bought that we aren't friends, hook, line, and sinker. You may have just saved our lives...for now.*

In the room, I try to think about what Sylvie has in mind. What her plan is for getting the key to the barn.

It feels like several hours before Brandon finally reappears and walks into the room. "Ryder and I are going out for a business meeting. Sylvie will be here to make sure you behave yourself. If I were you, I'd stay out of her way. She meant what she said about kicking the shit out of you. Never mess with a street chick." He laughs, then closes the door.

I stand impatiently at the door, like a racehorse waiting before the buzzer sounds and the gate opens.

The seconds seem like hours before I finally hear the front door open and close. With my hand on the doorknob, I force myself to wait, giving our captors enough time to get into the car and pull away. I try to calm myself and count slowly to one hundred before I open the door and sprint down the stairs.

When I get to the kitchen, there's the smell of soapy steam coming from the open bathroom door. Sophie hears me in the kitchen, and comes out of her bedroom. I study her swollen, bruised face, looking for a sign of hope. "Did you figure out a way to get into the barn?"

She leans her sore body against the door frame. "Are you trying to ask if I found a way to get Ryder's key?"

I nod.

Then, she raises her shaky hand and opens it. Shining brightly in the stream of light coming through the window is a gold key.

I close my eyes and bend over, resting my hands on my knees. I take a deep breath and thank God. "How did you get the key?"

She gestures to the open bathroom door. "Ryder took a shower before they left. I crept in and went through his pants."

"But if he caught you, he could've killed you."

She shakes her head. "Not could have. *Would* have."

I look at her in awe. She's the bravest woman I've ever known.

"We don't have long, Sophie. And Ryder and Brandon took the keys for both the car and the truck, which means that after I take the pictures, we'll have to escape on-foot."

"Okay. So, we need to go to the basement to hit the breakers?"

"Yes. At least if the guys come back before we can leave, the cameras will have been off."

I help Sylvie with putting on her sweater. Then she tells me to fetch a small leather waist bag that's hidden under the dresser. As instructed, I clip it around her waist. Something tells me that all the implicating information she's collected on Ryder is in that satchel.

As we walk to the basement, I notice that Sylvie is moving slowly, and I worry about how she'll make the long escape from the farmhouse on-foot.

Once we click off the breaker, the omnipresent dull hum in the house ceases. Sylvie opens her phone and checks the time. "It's 4:35. The sun will be setting soon, so at least we'll have the cover of darkness on our side."

Sylvie opts to take the photographs herself. Instead of letting me come inside the barn with her, she orders me to stand at the entrance and watch for any signs of Ryder and Brandon. My heart thumps and my eyes play tricks on me as I stare up the narrow dirt road.

It seems to take forever before Sylvie finally reappears. She doesn't say a word, but the expression on her face tells me everything. She looks like the cat who ate the canary.

"I take it you're satisfied?" I ask.

She grins. "More than."

"Now that you have what you need, can't we just call the cops from your phone?"

"This phone is mine. There are no minutes on it. The cell I used yesterday was one of Ryder's, and he took it with him when he left."

* * *

Dark angry clouds roll across the dusty sky as the last of daylight swiftly fades. We walk off the property and head up the long, narrow, dirt road.

Right away it's obvious that no matter what happens, Sylvie won't be able to run. The more we trudge along the road, the more she complains of pain on one side of her lower back. She doesn't like to be touched, I know that much about her, but after my nagging her for ten minutes, she finally lets me lift her sweater to look at her back.

I gasp when I see the fresh, shoe print-sized bruise. I tell her how bad it looks, and in two short words she ends the topic. "I'll heal."

We stop a few more minutes up the gravel road for Sylvie to catch her breath. I look around for any buildings in the surrounding farm fields where she can hide while I get help, but she quickly nixes that idea. "Ryder and Brandon would check every structure around if they were looking for us."

I start getting anxious when I look back at the farmhouse and notice that we haven't made it that far. It's mostly dark now, and the monsters could come back any time. Instead of watching where my feet step, my sole focus is on Sylvie and watching for Ryder's car.

Out of the blue, Sylvie's mood perks up and she starts talking about Faith, and how she can't wait to hold her without Ryder or his mother around. "After I get her back, I'm going to decorate her room with pink princesses and kittens." Sylvie laughs. "She's such a girl."

Even though her face is swollen and her lips are scabbed, there's a glow radiating from her.

"When you get her back, where will the two of you live?"

"Far away from here." She shakes her head. "I don't want Ryder or his family having anything to do with her."

"Maybe you'll become one of those moms that makes cookies for school events. Maybe you'll even join a parent group."

"Yeah, right. Can you see me in that role?"

We laugh.

"All I care about is being a good mom to my—"

There's a flash of light ahead as a vehicle turns off the pavement and onto the dirt road. I freeze.

"What is it?" Sylvie says.

I don't answer. I just point ahead.

"Shit! That's probably Ryder's car. We've got to hide."

We look around for a shelter, but all we see is a blueberry field next to the road. I grab Sylvie's arm and help her down the side of the gravel to the field. Even though blueberry season has long ended and all the fruit is gone, the leaves are bushy. If we get down low enough, we shouldn't be seen.

We crouch down in the dirt between a narrow row of plants just as the car passes and turns into the farm.

"It won't be long until they discover we're gone and come looking for us," Sylvie says.

Fear pushes adrenaline through my body. "Yeah, well, they're not looking for us yet. Let's go. That old motel is just on the other side of this field." I grab her arm and put it over my shoulder. I move head-first through the stiff plants, acting as a crutch for Sylvie. "You watch for Ryder and Brandon, and I'll keep us moving."

Using my shoulder and my head, I plow through the plants as fast as I can, until Sylvie groans, "They're coming."

I stop, look back, and see two figures with flashlights coming up the road.

"Oh no. Sylvie. We've got to hurry. You've got to muster all your strength and move forward. If they find us, we're dead."

Keeping our heads down, we work together and maneuver through the foliage. Both of us are out of breath and exhausted, and our gait eventually slows until our run has turned into a walk. Finally, Sylvie pats my shoulder as a way of telling me we need to stop.

When the noise of our bodies against the brush stops, the men's footsteps on the gravel becomes louder. "You go, Sophie," Sylvie whispers. "Leave me here."

I shake my head. "You're dreaming, girl. You're not giving up now. Think of little

Faith, and how devastated she'd be without her mama."

My words seem to motivate her. She suddenly gets a burst of power and moves faster than before. But her efforts are short-lived and within minutes, her breathing grows laboured again and she's grunting in pain.

Just as I reach around her waist to help her walk, one of the lights skims the tops of our heads. Immediately, we stop in our tracks, not breathing.

Brandon's voice booms out as if he's standing right beside us. "Let's go back and get the car. Those bitches could be on the paved road by now."

We peer up and see the flashlights turn back toward the house.

"Watch their lights and make sure they're not trying to trick us. I'll keep us moving."

The more we trudge, the darker the field gets, until it's hard to see where the earth ends and the night sky begins. Sylvie is weakening with every step, and from her weight, I am also waning.

Just as I'm about to take another step, I trip on a tall mound of dirt in front of us. Barely correcting our fall, I stumble and catch my footing. Then, I notice that the mound of dirt is actually the upslope to the paved road.

I maneuver Sylvie in front of me and push her up until she's standing on the road. Joining her, I quickly look back at the farmhouse for car headlights, but so far, nothing is coming.

Then, I look forward at the old motel. "We've got to hide." I help her across the road to the old building.

"They'll look for us here," Sylvie says as I sit her on the steps.

"They're going to look for us everywhere. But maybe there's a good hiding space in here."

She takes a few deep breaths. I wrap my arms around her. I'm just getting her to her feet when she points to the gravel road. "Look. They're coming."

I look up at the long stairs above us, then back at the nearing headlights. There's no way we're going to make it inside before they spot us.

I lift Sylvie. This time, instead of helping, she's limp, her body dead weight. Again, I look at the approaching car. I grit my teeth, fill my lungs with air, and somehow lift Sylvie under her arms and drag her to the top of the landing. I set her down on debris of painted-wood splinters and chunks of glass from the broken windows.

"Sophie, you need to take this, just in case." Sylvie unzips the satchel bag, reaches in, and pulls out a baggy with a phone inside. "It belonged to your friend Tessa. It's dead, but Brandon's prints should be all over it, as well as Ryder's."

"Thank you, Sylvie." I want to hug her and tell her how grateful I am, but this isn't the right time or place.

I look down just in time to see the car pull up and the doors open. Ryder jumps out of the passenger side and sprints toward the stairwell. Brandon isn't far behind him. I picture his handgun, and my legs weaken and shake.

Ryder latches on to Sylvie's legs and pulls her toward him. "You're dead now, bitch."

Sylvie moans when the first punch hits her. I try to kick him away, but he's sitting firmly on top of her and won't be moved. Another blow, and then another, and her face is soon covered in blood.

"Stop!" I scream, but his fists keep making contact with Sylvie's face.

Then, amidst the blows, I see Brandon trying to struggle past them.

His eyes briefly touch on mine and he grins maniacally. "You're next."

Sylvie is barely conscious, but when Ryder pulls his arm back to hit her again, I see Sylvie's hand move, feeling around the floor. I watch her grab a large shard of glass. Just as he leans forward to plow his fist into her again, her eyes open wide and she looks straight at him, then plunges the glass into his neck, a bloody smile tugging at her destroyed lips. Then, her eyes close and her head flops to the side.

Immediately, Ryder loses his power and sits back, grabbing his throat. He gurgles as blood spurts between his fingers.

Brandon finally maneuvers beside him, sees Ryder, then hollers, "What the fuck happened?"

I turn and look behind me at the row of doors. Then, as fast as I can, I run toward the last one. I push hard on the rotted wood and the frame cracks and breaks, allowing the door to swing open.

In a panic, I look around the room for anything that could serve as a weapon, but the unit has been gutted. Other than an old, rusted sink vanity, there's nothing.

When I hear his voice behind me, my heart sinks deep into my chest. There's no way past him, and I don't have the strength to fight. My body is exhausted, and my mind is crippled with fear. Whatever hope I had for surviving is quickly disappearing. Any dream I was holding onto about seeing Mom and Dad again fades.

I just hope it's quick. I hope he shoots me and I die fast. I don't want to suffer anymore.

I turn to face the monster. His shoulders are heaving, and his face is filled with psychotic rage.

I don't say anything. There's no point. I've pleaded with him before, and it did nothing.

He walks toward me as he cracks his knuckles. "This is going to be fun."

When he's only about a foot away, I close my eyes and ready myself for what's about to happen.

Then, out of the blue, a voice pierces through my nightmare. "On the ground, or I'll blow your fucking head off."

I open my eyes to see a large silhouette standing in the doorway of the room.

Brandon turns. "Who the hell are you?"

"I'm with the police, and you're dead unless you get down."

This can't be happening. I can't believe it.

Brandon slowly raises his hands. He looks like he's going to kneel on the floor, but then reaches around his back and pulls out the gun that was tucked into his pants.

There's a loud crack, and Brandon drops to the floor.

The silhouette walks slowly toward me. "Are you okay, Sophie?"

"You know me?" I stammer.

When he's directly in front of me, I recognize him. It's Darren, the man who came to the farmhouse the day I first passed a box of drugs.

"Who are you?"

"I'm a detective. Everything is going to be okay."

* * *

Flashing lights pulse against the exterior of the old motel as a circus of emergency vehicles crowd the small lot.

Darren sits me in the front seat of his black muscle car and holds my hand as I watch the ambulance take Brandon away on a stretcher.

With firemen standing behind them, paramedics feverishly try to revive Sylvie, but their efforts are unsuccessful. Soon after, both her body and Ryder's are covered in thin, white sheets.

Darren and I pull away from the old motel and follow behind a string of marked cop cars. As we drive through Abbotsford, I can't help thinking how small the city looks to me now.

Chapter Twelve

I never realized how much I missed the smell of this place. The same bouquet of dime-a-bucket perfume, mixed with the ever-present caustic stench of industrial cleaner.

I look at the time and smile. *I'm late again. Some things never change.*

I rush down the long white corridor toward my class. When I open the door and the professor glares at me, along with the room full of students, and even though a year has passed, I know I'm exactly where I'm supposed to be.

While in intensive therapy, I decided to become a Social Service worker, so I can one day help people in similar situations that I was in. I've attended a few events where Darren was the guest speaker, warning people about the deadly ramifications of being involved in the drug trade.

Brandon only spent a week in pre-trial before he was murdered by his cellmate when they learned he'd killed two young women. Ironically, he was strangled.

Much to my parents' dismay, I never had the tattoo of his name removed from my body. Instead, I keep it as a reminder of what I went through, so I can remember my experience and share it authentically with others.

Sometimes, when my mind flashes back to the abandoned motel and the horrible events of that night, I think about Sylvie. How her life could've been if she had lived. I picture Faith, a fair-skinned little girl with curly red hair like her mommy's, and hope that she knows how hard her mother fought to be with her, and how much she was loved.

I think about Tess. I hope she's happy where she is, and that she knows how sorry I am. And I hope she's proud of the path I've taken toward helping girls like us.

The End

Readers we need you.

Please leave a review, even a one liner counts, and has a big influence on our future sales.

Jay Lang books also published by BWL Publishing Inc.

Hush
Shatter
Shiver
Storm
The Cove
Impulse
The Immoral
Deadly Ties
Run Baby Run
The Gooey-Duck Fountain

Jay Lang grew up on the ocean, splitting her time between Read Island and Vancouver Island before moving to Vancouver to work as a TV, film and commercial actress. Eventually she left the industry for a quieter life on a live-a-board boat, where she worked as a clothing designer for rock bands. Five years later she moved to Abbotsford to attend university. There, she fell in love with creative writing and wrote five novel manuscripts in a year. She spends her days hiking and drawing inspiration for her writing from nature.

BWL Publishing

bwlpublishing.ca